Bad Hombres

& Nasty Women

I0646213

Anthology by The Raving Press
Edited by Gabriel H. Sanchez
and Isaac Chavarria

Cover Art by Dmitry Borshch
from "America's Presidential Race 2016: 16 collages from Russia"
"Lillian Locks the Door" by Anders Carlson-Wee previously published in *Forklift, Ohio*

ISBN-13: 978-0998996509

DEDICATION

The greatest country on earth deserves the greatest artists, the greatest writers, the greatest poets, and the greatest heroes. We want to dedicate this anthology to all those *Bad* (GOOD) Hombres and *Nasty* (AWESOME) Women of our great nation who are speaking out against all forms of discrimination and abuse: be it bigotry, racism, misogyny, and bullying in any way.

We received an overwhelming response to our call for literature for this project, which took us by surprise. We expected the response to be localized to our region of the U.S. (South Texas) but the response came from all parts of the country. From the East Coast to the West Coast, the North and the South. The answer was loud and passionate. America the great is alive and well, and eager to lend its voice to the cause for justice and the American way.

This anthology has become one of the most important projects we have undertaken. But the most significant aspects of it are the contributions by the artists and writers who submitted the works that were selected to appear in this collection. Thanks to our friend Xanath Caraza for a powerful introduction. Although Xanath originally wrote it in Spanish, we felt that her exceedingly well crafted preface deserved to be included in English as well.

We have no doubt that the reader will agree that the *Bad Hombres & Nasty Women* anthology is one of the most significant books of the year if not the decade. Thank you for reading. Please share this book and its message widely.

From the Editors

CONTENTS

Phillip Bannowsky

INTRODUCTION

by Xanath Caraza

(Translated by Gabriel H. Sanchez)

Poetry and narrative as dialectic processes are a constant transmutation that like a wind or water vortex produces a linguistic synthesis in direct response, in most instances, to the political and contextual manifestations of our age. This anthology represents a response to an erroneous adscription leveled at chicanas and chicanos, latinas and latinos in the United States. It is a cleansing of—and an appeal against—an imposed set of unfounded proclamations, utilizing words to wash them away by reclaiming and repurposing the two concepts "Bad Hombres" & "Nasty Women." In turn, poets and writers responded to the call by using the new concepts as a catalyst for the creation of potent poetry and prose laden with social commentary.

We should celebrate the cultural heritage which chicanos, chicanas, latinos, latinas have imparted to this nation as much as we should celebrate every wave of immigrants which has reached our shores and has contributed to the formation of what we know as these United States. How to declare this country as "mine" if the adjective qualifiers that pretend to portray our likeness are nothing more than minimizing pejoratives? How to feel as part of the greater whole who share the roots set upon this land when our officials fail to celebrate the contributions of the immigrant in a dignified manner? Therein lies the origin of this anthology of poetry and prose; a space where poets and narrators are conjured to reclaim, respond, and recreate the representations of immigrants, latinas, latinos, chicanas, chicanos, the plight of women, class distinction, and many more social ills which are central to our present reality.

In this anthology, poets and writers depict a vision and a collective sentiment that cannot be silenced. Silence could never be the solution, for it is the written and enunciated word, which like an incantation, counters and abolishes hurtful and misplaced descriptions. These poets and prose writers are brimming with intent and "*ganas*" [fervor] to bring about change for our present and future generations. The hard-fought victories earned by chicanos, chicanas, latinos, latinas in the United States cannot be eradicated by nonsensical positing. That is why when readers immerse themselves in the pages within this book they will discover the strength of the poet. They will fuse with the poetry and prose written primarily in English, with a few lines in Spanish, and on occasion, writings interspersed with code switching between the two languages.

We hear Edward Vidaurre say "we can be brown together." I can relax and be myself. We translate the lines that read, "she can wear rebozos and I / can get tattoos of feathered hair Chicanas." We are who we are and it is right that we use the *rebozo* [shawl] as a symbol to honor previous generations of women, specifically *las adelitas*, those who formed part of the Mexican Revolution. Seres Jaime Magaña writes, "We see that you intended to expel the love from our lives" channeling the strength and the goodness of the people, of *la Raza*. He adds that despite all that is being imposed on us "We will shine through with our multicolored eyes;" that specter of light shall cause this burdensome darkness to rise up off our backs floating upward like smoke plumes taking away with it all prejudice until they disappear.

In Mónica Alvarez's lament we feel the perils of a journey to reach Los Angeles. We experience in her words the great suffering that many have endured in that lengthy peregrination, "The putrid smell of rotten corpses / danced around the meadow, / where the virgin flowers / turned away / so their silky petals / would not get tarnished / by the filthy stroke / of blood-soaked wind." We sing along with "Song for America" by Fernando Esteban Flores and shout a loud chorus, "Sweat in America's factories / Wait on America's tables / Fight in America's wars." And then we dance as we reclaim our identity to the tune of "gabachita's corrido. / a bit tejana, rancherita, a bit hip hop, pop a bit classical, antigüita" by Priscilla Celina Suarez, who upon listening to a song while in the waiting room at a dentist's office is moved to reflect upon the love of her people; of those who have been lost and those who have been buried; of those who have made her who she is: a proud chicana who exudes the heritage of *la raza* through her pores.

Between the lines of prose tales within, this anthology culminates with images fed through different experiences and observations of unjust situations visited upon our people. Such tales as Phillip Bannowsky's "Jacobo Gets the Good Job" which with incisive images leads us by the hand from the first line to a place of work where the ICE agents arrive unannounced; something many of us are intimately familiar with. With agile storytelling, Bannowsky keeps us on edge throughout, narrating the interior world of the protagonist existing in his own exterior reality as if caught between parallel universes until that moment that takes him by surprise; that prompts him to flee; that compels him to think of his fellow workers from Guatemala and Ecuador, of hardworking family men like himself. We escape alongside the protagonist until the early morning sun dazzles our eyes and finds us as it shines through corn plant leaves. There, in our last refuge, a cutting voice, like a machete, asks: "Amigo, do you speak English?"

It is an open-ended question. It is posed at the world for posterity. This world where friends should be welcome and not condemned. We are the cornerstone of this country. Our previous generations have planted every form of fruit and vegetable which adorn our tabletops. We are our daily bread, and that is what this anthology proclaims. Bad Hombres & Nasty Women is a fervent declaration, a handful of fresh but potent words which exalt our perspective, vindicate our ancestors, our parents, mothers, fathers, brothers, sisters and over all else, our youth. Let us rise and break through, breaching a space where we may call things by their true names.

Xánath Caraza
Kansas City, MO

INTRODUCCIÓN
por Xanath Caraza

La poesía y narrativa como procesos dialécticos son un constante devenir que como remolinos de agua y de viento producen una síntesis lingüística que responde, muchas veces, a la situación política y contexto de nuestro tiempo. Esta antología responde a una adscripción errónea que se ha dado a las chicanas y chicanos, las latinas y latinos en los Estados Unidos. Esta antología limpia y reivindica lo que se ha querido imponer y lava con palabras lo que se ha dictado sin fundamento. No se detiene ahí, retoma estos dos conceptos, Bad Hombres & Nasty Women, los reclama y los hace creación pura; los poetas y escritores contestan y los usan como catalizador para crear una cascada de poemas y relatos de comentario social.

Celebrar las herencias culturales que los chicanos, chicanas, latinos, latinas que han contribuido a este país, es lo que todos deberíamos hacer constantemente. De igual manera celebrar cada ola de migrantes que ha llegado a los Estados Unidos y ha hecho de este país lo que entendemos como tal.

Cómo decir este país es mío si los adjetivos calificativos que nos retratan son minimizadores y peyorativos. Cómo sentir que las raíces de este suelo son nuestras si no se celebran las contribuciones de los migrantes de manera digna por los medios oficiales. Éste es el origen de esta antología de poesía y narrativa, un espacio donde se conjuntan poetas y narradores para reclamar, contestar y recrear las percepciones de migrantes, latinas, latinos, chicanas, chicanos, la condición de la mujer, clase social y otros tantos temas que son centrales a nuestra realidad actual.

Esta antología está hecha de reacciones constructivas que exponen la visión y sentimientos que jóvenes poetas y narradores no pueden callar. El silencio no es la solución sino la palabra escrita y enunciada para, como un conjuro, deshacer las descripciones equivocadas y hasta dolorosas. Estos poetas y narradores están llenos de ganas, de intenciones de lograr un cambio para las generaciones de hoy y las futuras. El duro camino y lugar ganado por los chicanos, chicanas, latinos, latinas en los Estados Unidos no puede ser erradicado por comentarios sin sentido. Es por eso que cuando el lector se compenetra en las páginas de esta antología descubre la fuerza de los poetas. Se vuelve uno con la poesía y narrativa escrita en su mayoría en inglés con poemas también en español y en ocasiones cambios de códigos lingüísticos.

Escuchamos a Edward Vidaurre decir "we can be brown together" me puedo relajar y ser quien soy, traducimos entre líneas, "she can wear rebozos and I / can get tattoos of feathered hair Chicanas". Somos quien somos y está bien usar rebozo como un símbolo para honrar las previas generaciones de mujeres, específicamente a las adelitas, las que formaron parte de la Revolución mexicana. Seres Jaime Magaña dice "We see that you intended to expel the love from our lives" y reclama la bondad y la fuerza de la gente, de la Raza; y agrega que a pesar de todo lo que se quiere imponer, "We will shine through with our multicolored eyes", ese espectro de luz permitirá que esta oscuridad impuesta se esfume para que los prejuicios también desaparezcan.

En el lamento de Mónica Alvarez sentimos el doloroso camino para llegar a Los Ángeles. Sufrimos con sus palabras lo que tantos han experimentado en ese largo andar, "The putrid smell of rotten corpses / danced around the meadow, / where the virgin flowers / turned away / so their silky petals / would not get tarnished / by the filthy stroke / of blood-soaked wind". Cantamos con "Song for America" de Fernando Esteban Flores y repetimos en voz alta "Sweat in America's factories / Wait on America's tables / Fight in America's wars". Al tiempo que bailamos, también reclamamos nuestra identidad con el "gabachita's corrido. / a bit tejana, rancherita, / a bit hip hop, pop / a bit classical, anigüita" de Priscilla Celina Suarez, a quien una canción que escucha en el consultorio del dentista le hace reflexionar sobre el amor por su gente, por los que ha perdido y hasta enterrado y que la han llevado a ser quien ella es, una chicana con mucho orgullo, que transpira la herencia de la raza en la piel.

Entre líneas de narrativa, los relatos, esta antología culmina con imágenes alimentadas por diferentes experiencias u observaciones de situaciones injustas experimentadas por nuestra gente. Como en el relato de Phillip Bannowsky, "Jacobo Gets the Good Job" que con imágenes incisivas nos lleva de la mano, desde la primera línea, al lugar de trabajo donde los agentes de ICE llegan sin aviso, como sabemos sucede en múltiples ocasiones. Su habilidad para contar nos tiene en tensión y de forma paralela narra sobre el mundo interior del protagonista y su mundo exterior, ese momento que lo toma por sorpresa, que lo hace escapar, que lo hace pensar en sus compañeros de trabajo de Guatemala, de Ecuador, de gente de familia, dedicada al trabajo. Nos hace escapar con el protagonista hasta que despunta la mañana y los primeros rayos de sol nos deslumbran entre las hojas de plantas de maíz. Ahí, cuando creemos estar a salvo, una voz afilada, como un machete, le pregunta, "Amigo, do you speak English?"

La pregunta queda abierta. La lanza al mundo. A este mundo donde los amigos y amigas deben ser bien recibidos y no condenados. Somos el fundamento de este país. Nuestras previas generaciones han sembrado cada fruta y verdura que hay en nuestras mesas, somos el pan nuestro de cada día y eso es lo que esta antología reclama. Bad Hombres & Nasty Women es un grito lleno de ganas, un puñado de palabras frescas y fuertes que ponen en perspectiva, reivindican a nuestros ancestros, a nuestros padres, madres, hermanos y sobre todo a nuestra juventud. Hay que abrir brecha y llamar a las cosas por su verdadero nombre.

Xánath Caraza

Kansas City, MO

Bad
Poetry

LILLIAN LOCKS THE DOOR
Anders Carlson-Wee

Don't worry about your shoes:
aint nothin you can track
in the door I aint killed before.
Never had a lock till the freeway
came through. Suddenly a gun's missin
from my pickup, tools from the shed.
Go ahead, open the blinds.
Them's apples on the north end,
grapes on the west, tomatoes
out back and corn beyond that.
Goat milk sells as pet food
but people know to drink it.
I gotta laugh to have you here—
been tryin to get rid of men
altogether. Got this double bolt
the same summer they laid
that freeway. Aint tryin to lock you in,
just makin sure the rest stays out.
Don't worry, I never had to kill
nobody. Wanted to kill plenty,
thought about killin even more.
And now with my stuff goin missin
in the night—makes me feel crazy,
but the only crazy thing I ever done
was get hitched in Hawaii once.
And Vegas another once.
I figured it was love and I'd worry
about the rest later. Well, the rest
showed up. Now I keep busy
with the plants and animals.
Men: the pretty girls can have em.

BAD VATO C/S NASTY RUCA
Edward Vidaurre

She looks nice, *gruesa, y pues*
I'm attracted
To that type

Oh don't even go there!
She's a hardcore queer chicana
She'll tear you down
She's fucking intelligent
She has a kid
She doesn't need a man.

I like that.
We can steal nopales
On our walks through town
She can wear *rebozos* and I
Can get tattoos of feathered hair
Chicanas with lazy eyes
We can be brown together

She can quote *La Gloria*, and I can
Eat *huevos con salchicha* for breakfast
She can rearrange our finances
Y yo le enseño como se bailan
Those oldies but goodies,
Pegaditos los dos so I can inhale
Her olorcito a café con leche

We can grow old together
And watch our *placasos* on our
arms turn into
Historic monuments
Una chicana, y un poeta.

FIRST THEY CAME
Don Mathis
(with apologies to Martin Niemöller)

First they came for the Snowflakes,
and I did not speak out —
Because I was not a Snowflake.

Then they came for the Nasty Women,
and I did not speak out —
Because I was not a Nasty Woman.

Then they came for the Bad Hombres,
and I did not speak out —
Because I was not a Bad Hombre.

Then they came for me —
and there was no one left to speak for me.

FUCK ME
PW Covington
dedicated to Sean Gregory Buttram

Fuck me
Fuck me for being
A white, American, male
And hearing more of MY voice
Echoed in rolled "r's" and tildes
Than in "My Country, 'tis of Thee"
Fuck me

Fuck me for refusing to stand for the flag
Or salute all that star-spangled splendor
Fuck me
For having sworn to and learned
The lies that lay beneath every war
Fuck me, for I know
The cold, perfect
Compliance of killing
Fuck me

Fuck me for not being
The kind of "Honest, hard-working, man"
That
"Feeds his family, any way that he can"
Through 80 hour weeks, and calloused hands
Fuck me for rejecting such scams
For making higher demands
And toiling for sunrise
In a cold, dark, land
Fuck me

Fuck me for preferring borders
And outcasts
Fringes, frontiers, and edges
For rejecting the center
Where dreams go to die
Where hate goes to hide
Fuck me

Fuck me for living
A white, American, man
For wanting to see the past left behind
For finding no kinship with my klan or kind
For grasping at hope
Not clinging to rage
Fuck me

THE PEOPLE UNITED
Seres Jaime Magaña

We see that you've decided to distance yourself from us
That you've raised a wall between two peoples who love each other
And they are brothers
A wall built from grudges, accusations,
And arrogance
We see that you intend to expel the love from our lives

You must believe that we surrender easily.

You ignore that we haven't been influenced
By sadness, or hatred, or fear
We are born from holiday
From the wind blowing with the scent of wheat
Of nights of hot chocolate,
Of mescal,
From skies lit by fireworks
And our joyful and tranquil heart knows that there is still room
For both of us

We will knock down the border
That supposed testimony of power
Which all it's good for to cover the sun
We will knock down the border
And we will remind you that your streets
Will forever carry the taste of our union

Of course it's not stubbornness
We can easily turn our backs
If it were not that we still believe in each other

The American people
With outstretched hands
Opened their doors
And welcomed me
I cannot see them as my enemy

No matter how many bricks you stack
You can still hear our heart pulsating inside
Like when two lovers lie their ears over their chest

And with their heartbeat tell their history
Drawing in the clouds a history together
Discovering in every word that they are history
Now this abyss intends to make us mute

We will not bind to our forehead that veil of black and white
We will shine through with our multicolored eyes

Speak, listen to us, talk to us
Do not aim your arms at us

Because what steals
What Abuses
The insensitive
The dishonest
The foolish
They are also our enemies.

We will knock down that border
Of prejudice
Of isolation
We will knock it down and forget it
Things like that aren't missed by anyone

Do not build your wall anymore

Tell me where you want to go
When you block all your roads?

I want to reach you
And show you the world that awaits us
If we work together

We will knock down the border
We will not climb it, we will not cross it
We will completely collapse it
And we will remind you what it means to love

And together
While the gentle breeze with the scent of cane
Caresses our hair
We will drink, while we forget
That which could have divided us

POOR OLD LEANDRO
Jose Sanchez

LENCHO: Oye, did you hear about poor old Leandro?

LALO: No. Que paso?

LENCHO: He's an American citizen!

LALO: Que what?!!
El era puro Mexican! He didn't want to go to the USA!

LENCHO: I know - but listen - this all happened because he got fired from his job at the aduana.

LALO: Oh, that's too bad.

LENCHO: No that's good.
Once he got fired, he discovered his true calling.

LALO: Oh, that's great!

LENCHO: No, that's not good, because he didn't have a license for his true calling (computer technology), so he took a job with a shady company.

LALO: Oh that's too bad.

LENCHO: Turned out to be good. It was a company that was working on the cutting edge of 3-D printing!

LALO: What good luck!

LENCHO: Turned out to be bad luck. He was printing an order of guns for the narco-terroristas, when his machine exploded!

LALO: Oh, no, that's terrible!

LENCHO: It turned out to be the best thing that ever happened to him.
The explosion catapulted him right over the Rio to the other side!

LALO: So, they made him an American!

LENCHO: Of course, not! They arrested him!

LALO: Oh, no! That's terrible!

LENCHO: He just wanted to come home, but he was lucky he didn't.

LALO: What happened?

LENCHO: When they found out that he had blown up that shady company, they gave him an award and he was deported with honor!

LALO: Fantastic!

LENCHO: No, terrible. Now the narco-terroristas were after him.

LALO: What did he do?

LENCHO: What could he do? He swam across!

LALO: How did he get to be a US citizen like that?

LENCHO: Easy - a few doctored documents - papeles y papeles y papeles - a convenient second cousin - and now he gets to live high on the hog in America!

Food stamps!

Medicaid!

Obamacare!

Special treatment!

Kid gloves!

Pampered lifestyle!

AHHHHH!

Un mundo raro
by Mónica Alvarez

"les diré que llegué de un mundo raro que no sé del dolor que triunfé en el amor y que nunca he llorado"

-José Alfredo Jiménez

I stood on a hill facing the Rio Grande
staring at the obscurity of the future
under a pale moon that watches me watching her
from this hybrid town that lies at the heart of the Texas borderlands.

The putrid smell of rotten corpses
danced around the meadow,
where the virgin flowers
turned away
so their silky petals
would not get tarnished
by the filthy stroke
of blood-soaked wind
carrying stories from southern countries,
the resilient tongue of the Other
attempting to reach their immaculate ears.

I stretched out my arms
trying to scratch away
the fear that leaks
from the wall of never-ending sorrows.
My hands soaked in bloody tears
that echoed the piercing clamor
of suffering mothers who lost their voices
calling out the names of their missing sons,
decomposed souls feeding coyotes in the middle of nowhere.
Calling out the names of their missing daughters,
bodies of lust made a wooden cross by patriarchal desires.

As I scraped the hatred off the steel fence
I dreamt that the metal bars melted in shame,
washed away by an unforgiving river made of

tears and dreams and strength and faith

                                    and death.

A maguey in the distance
reminds me of those bohemian eyes;
embriagantes y punzantes,
a memory that haunts
my sleepless nights.

I let myself go
lost in the deserted vastness of the unknown.
Ephemeral hopes inside my heart,
evoking the evening where
the rain took our goodbye.
I sink my feet in the river
trying to turn my soul to song,
a hummingbird searching for
"un mundo raro"
where the water is peace
where the wind is not fire
where your eyes do not leave
y el amor es un sueño dorado.

NEIGHBORHOOD
Bri Ianniello

Gardeners sweating
in fancy greenery with
Spanish dictionaries right at hands.
Friendly nods, efforts and understanding.

Displays laden with galletas,
fragile grandpas selling tamales.
Omnipresent pyramids of fresh produce:
oranges, avocados and cilantro.

Hola, ¿qué tal? A sunny smile hovers over dark,
wooden tables polished with dedication.
Endless chatters, laughter and love.
Bitter-sweet lemon scent permeates the air.

What will the future hold?

Lost Angels Crossing (was: Los Angeles)
Sticky tables, pale fries and hamburgers.

Chipotle's beans faded history then
Hollywood Boulevard sin Superman

Carlos Estevez relaxing at Cancun beach
Charlie Sheen has left the States — doing as they preach.

Iñárritu off to new shores — settling the rant
in Canada's forests; Birdman meets Revenant.

Truth to be told:

We don't need no ban, no hate and no wall,
but justice and human rights for all.
California without Mexico?
Gee — thank you, but no.

A WITHERING REIGN

Inspired by The Bayeux Tapestry 1077
Debbie Guzzi

Clouds, top stitched with crows, smother a cruel sky.
The tapestry of morn captioned with flying glyphs
glowers at the assignations of allies?
Across the tundra, a Russian bear lopes
standing to shred the welkin with claw and
fang while the eagle sleeps with the Kremlin's gifts.
On the bleached bones of the weak, the eagle gnaws
its baser side feasts on the kills of others.
Ruled by gold, its Aryan leaders once abhorred
demonstrate the state of hate between brothers.
Let rebels rise, Betsys with needles in their hands
to mend the standard of our founding mothers.
Pierce the sky at this cruel time, right demands
the return of light and justice to this land.

SONG FOR AMERICA
XVII

Fernando Esteban Flores

Some Bad Hombres
—Donald Trump

Leap tall border walls
In a single bound
Ground America's buildings
Build America's railways
Glean America's crops
Wash iron mop sweep
Keep America *squeaky* clean
Tend to America's gardens
Construct America's homes
Collect America's garbage
Service America's cars
Sweat in America's factories
Wait on America's tables
Fight in America's wars
Die in America's wars
Steal American jobs
Snubbed American citizenship
Dubbed the welfare class
Called criminals & rapists
Dark & undesirable
American as dirt

I mean those are some bad hombres
We need to get them out

At Seventy, Stop Building the Fence
Steven Ray Smith

A new Stonewall Jackson
fought the Mexicans back across the Rio Grande.
Realizing the rivulet wasn't grand
enough to hold them back, he built a short inept fence
that did nothing except block the view of the water.

Baby Mexicans and their poor young parents
continued to arrive daily for the paychecks
he offered them to cook his Mexican
food and weedwack his weeds, but because
Stonewall did not want to see
them after he swallowed the enchilada or the sprinklers
sparged his gloriosas, he boosted the fence.

At last the unattended weeds began boosting
the foundation of his gilded chateau. What to do?

Stonewall's votaries, those bedfellows beefed
about the squeeze on middle-class comfort,
urged him to keep his fence and give some
breathing room to their pauperizing quantile.
His adversaries and fellow gastronomes
urged him to keep their tacos cheap, hence no fence.

Only another septuagenarian, having finally learned
that no engineering can channel an entire Rio
Grande, said throw open your propylaeum, lest
purslane and spurge
overgrow you.

Refugee

Ana M. Fores Tamayo

My soul into pieces,
I see the barbed wire
ripping metal against skin.
Crying tears of blood,
I hear gunshots in the vacuumed silence
of the gang's Salva Maratrucha.
I push him under the fence
but my son cries.
No matter:
I do it because
I love him.
We walk walk walk…
hours and hours on the rotted roads
of the Coyotes,
days, weeks, a month, hand in hand:
we go, sick —
without eating,
without drinking,
without speaking.
Or when we speak, we do so crying,
because there is nothing left for more.
Where did my little son's childhood go?
When did he lose it?
Is it when he saw his uncle fall by a bullet
meant for his mother?
The eternity of hell
has bridged our path,
and so we cross the border
reaching the river.
We travel in rafts;
I am the walking dead
with my little son in my arms.
We give up
in that land of darkness
as we throw ourselves at their feet —
the faceless border patrol: no image, no semblance.
And I say, whispering,
"I am afraid."

II
I remember the black eyes
of my brother,
parted, glazed over,
blood bursting his bowels,
my grandmother screaming
run, girl, run,
It is you they want,
it is your sex,
your power as woman,
your way of saying no.
Still I hear the distant gunfire
as I listen to the voice of
my grandmother once again:
go with your child before
they kill you, she says.
And the present shatters nightmares
that produce even more assaults:
I perceive a mercenary,
burning flames...
Shock catapults me to the present.
Border patrol interrogate me,
"Will you return?"
And I say, sarcastically:
"I want to see my country,
I want to hear the
raging shootouts,
I want to see the maras
assaulting one another,
kill man kill.
I want to see my dear dead brother,
I want to be my grandmother's star of light
crying crying.
I want to see the blood bedazzle
the green of my rugged mountains,
the stones of my pebbled streets,
the river water flowing,
but all is red red
blood blood
Cry cry."
"Run, girl, run:
you are our only salvation.

Take your son away,
deliver him from oh, this horror."
So I hear that panicked voice,
my grandmother's dreaded words,
but I want never to remember…
What is it, girl?
Asks the agent, mean and foul.
I am afraid, Policeman Sir.
I am afraid.
But still, he does not want to hear.

III
He grabs me strongly, with brute force,
bashing us, this bully ICE man.
He knocks us down, thrashing, bellicose.
My son falls from my protection,
my trembling little boy.
He drags us, this inhuman monster —
forcing us toward the glaring lights:
incandescent, blinding,
their flare piercing round and round.
He imprisons us in an old dogcatcher
screeching sirens screaming,
slatted with thick metal,
Is this cop car made for dogs?
But no.
Cloaked in clothes drenched by an icy river
and the key deception of the dwarfed hole
to which the armed guards cage us,
we arrive at a bleak, sterile prison:
insensible, aseptic,
sanitized of all damned godliness,
they freeze us both
while we embrace each other,
my little boy and me.
The warmth of mother and son
is always enough to take away
the cold from smiting bastards,
but not so when it comes to disarming
perverse spirits,
to striking fear in the most evil.
I huddle closely with my son,
crying crying…

IV

We arrive to our cell
with other mothers, other defenseless children.
Oh, fluorescent lights wail
both day and night.
Meals reminisce disgust.
There is no life
beyond today.
The guards despise us,
try to humiliate me
as if it were I
who would have done the crime,
as if it were I
who would have hurt
my brother
instead of the one who's running
for her life…
And I sense my brother
all a man,
a memory
with blue sky tie,
cerulean whispers
dressed in bleached white linen.
Then I watch him walk away
slowly, innocently,
with limbs of timeless oak.
But is this
the memory of my son,
or is this my brother come alive again?
Will this be a dream
from here or from beyond?

V

We spend months in a cornucopia
of agonies,
a monotony of routine days
where nothing happens,
because everything is deception,
everything is artificial,
everything is mad.
Finally comes the day when we talk
to a commissioner,

an official of that Machiavellian ICE:
we must explain our fear.
This man looks at us indifferently,
tells me, not believing,
Why are you here, girl?
Have you come to steal our food?
And I think of my dear brother,
slaughtered, in cold blood,
a battalion filled with drugs
despoiling my sacred land,
yet surfacing in this free expanse,
and I think of the vegetation
they demolished
to undertake what ravages
my country
nowadays.
I think of the land,
of the lives,
of the blood they steal from me...
I think of my son,
of my dear dead brother,
of us — the women they have raped;
I think of my beloved people,
of my homeland — wrecked, destroyed.
And then I see the migra,
I look toward the agent,
those men who work for ICE,
asking scornfully
if I think I might assault them,
so I tell them, bitterly:
Yes, since you disdain
to mock me,
I come explicitly for vengeance.
I come so you can suffer
delighting in my criminality,
I come so that you understand
that guilt, of oh, so much my pain.
Beware:
the woman raped, her brother dead.
Contemplate oh these transgressions,
the threats, the misery,
the massacres, the death in life:
this is my beloved country.

And then, remember me —
detail by bloody detail;
reflect on what it is I represent,
and memorize these tears of blood
when you laugh at every refugee.

UNA TARDE IN THE DENTISTA'S WAITING ROOM

Priscilla Celina Suarez

Tocan una canción de Ramon Ayala.
"nada me importa" I hear him
croon from the speakers outside
a Progresso dentista's office. I stare
        outside the glass doors
        into a busy world
        where sombreros and bootleg cd's
        block my view from the dusty & dirty road.
I hear Lucerito's voice
but can't quite make out the song.
I smell the scent of a dr.'s office
making me nauseas
with the fear of needles.
        I close my eyes for a few seconds,
        and in those seconds
        I swallow Ramon's music
        with the sincerity of the gente
making up this gabachita's corrido.
        a bit tejana, rancherita,
        a bit hip hop, pop,
        a bit classical, antigüita,
        but a lot, a lot Tex Mex fresa.
Tesorito, my favorite word in Ramon's
vocabulary. *Tesorito* I repeat and
think back to an overload of faces.
My tesoritos, songwriters de mi alma.
        The air conditioner's vent
        throws me cool air
        on this typical afternoon
        of asoleada's and aguas frescas.
Mis motivos are, no matter where
I go, to carry this feeling
of being home, of the love
I still carry for people I've
loved and lost, buried and died for,
to carry them
as they've carried me.

LATE AFTERNOONS
Lynne S Viti

I finished my degree, found a teaching post
at a good university, my chairman, a tall, broad
Iowa-bred guy of sixty with big hands, big feet,
Told big stories about flying in the bombing raids
On Dresden during the war. He seemed kind,
jovial, devoted to the work.
He made sure I met all the right people at conferences,
encouraged me to publish more, he raved
in his observation reports about my classes.
He shared details of his
grown children's good new, he praised his wife.
But one late afternoon in his office, when everyone else
Had gone home, when we were talking about plans
For summer school courses, when we had finished
Talking, when I had glanced at the bits of peanut shells
And husks on his desk, he suddenly rose from his chair,
The heavy green metal desk no longer between us,
Came at me fast, a strong arm swept around me, he
Began to pull me close. He said he had
"earned the right to do this." Stunned,
I leaned away, he pulled me in tighter. I ducked out
of this bear's embrace, grabbed
my coat and book bag, ran upstairs to the lobby,
my heart thumping. The night custodian
slowly pushed his wide dust mop across the floor.
Shy, a man of few words, he smiled weakly at me,
Told me it was time to go home, his usual farewell.
When I got to my car my hand shook
as I tried the key in the ignition switch.
I didn't tell anyone for years.

Yes, yes, my mother schooled me well,
said if this ever happens,
Kick him in the privates, or use
Your knee to the groin—as hard as you can.
I trusted this oaf, mistook him for a mentor.
Now I see it was all training me for that moment,
when students had disappeared to their dorms,
Faculty had packed up their lecture notes, headed home.
He had handled me as he would a feral cat,

slowly brought from the wild into his sphere of influence
With bits of food, kind words, shelter from weather.
It's been decades. He's dead now, or
I'd have a few words with that
sonofabitch.

Nasty

Art Gallery

Monster in a Dress Shop, No. 6
Christine Stoddard

Untitled
by Paul Luikart

Weathered Reports:
Trump Surrogate Quote from the Underground 19
a text-based art collaboration between
writer Mark Blickley and fine arts photographer Amy Bassin

Short-fingered vulgarian?
Thirty pictures on Trump,
the vulgarian whose fingers are not short
No. 1
(from "America's Presidential Race 2016:
16 collages from Russia")
by Dmitry Borshch

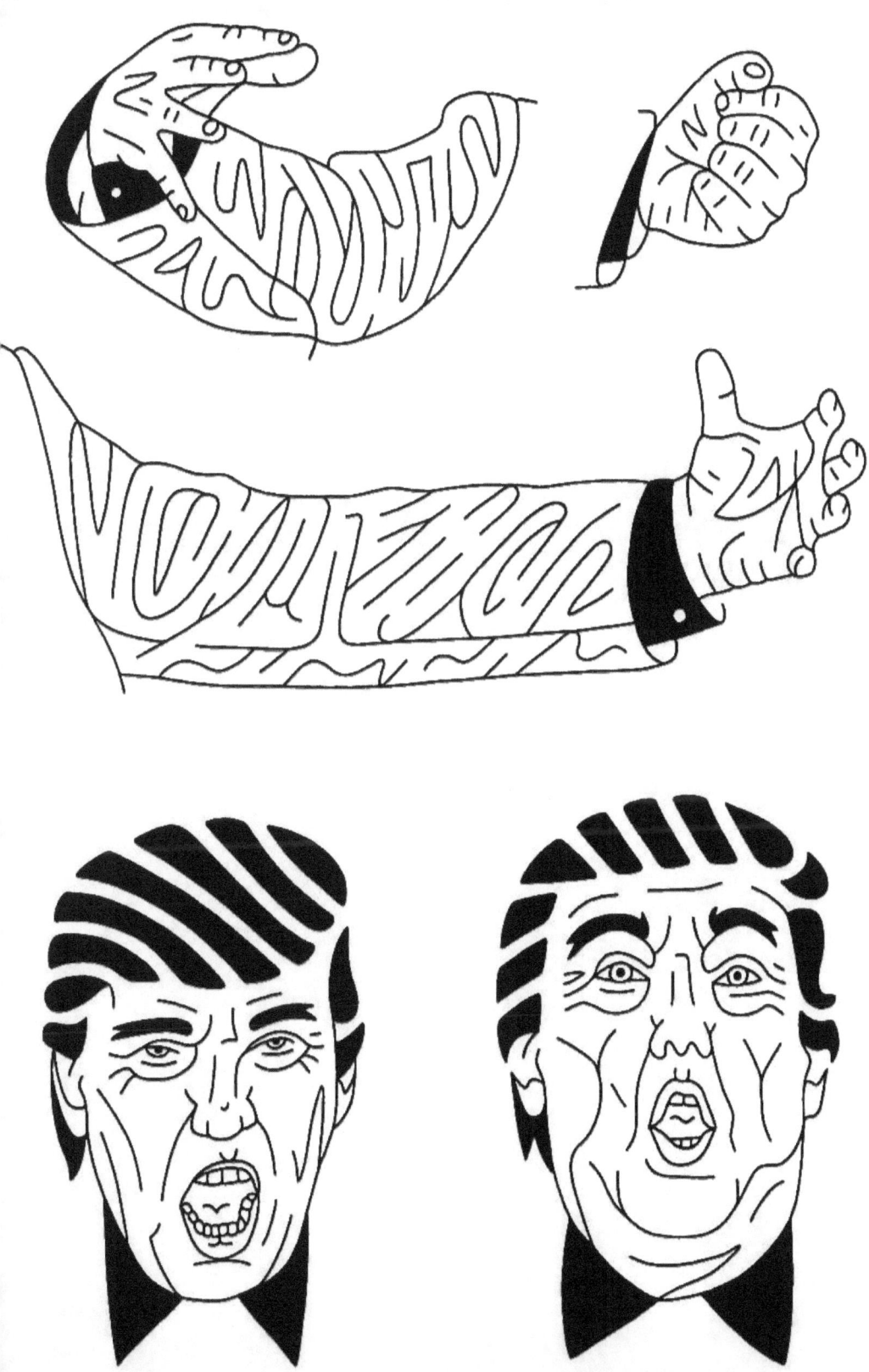

Deplorable
Prose

NUMERO CUARENTA Y CINCO
By Bruce Harris

Baseball commissioner Frank Sullivan stood behind the microphone on a sunny summer day in Cooperstown, New York. The swelling crowd leaned closer toward the stage as Sullivan prepared to introduce the newest member of Baseball's revered Hall of Fame.

"Ladies and gentlemen," began Sullivan, "It is my great pleasure and honor on this historic occasion to welcome to the stage a man who has hit not only more homeruns than anyone in baseball before him, he also holds the records for the ten longest measured homeruns in baseball history!" Sullivan waited for the applause and shouts to quiet down. "Without further ado, the newest member of baseball's Hall of Fame, and the lone 2077 inductee, Ricardo Carbonero!"

The once shy Mexican-born slugger rose from his seat and shook Sullivan's hand. The commissioner faded into the background, as Carbonero smiled and with continuous nodding of his head and clasped hands, bowed to the crowd in thanks. The cheering continued for nearly ten minutes. Carbonero signaled them to stop, but each time he tried, the applause increased. Finally, it was his turn to speak.

"Thank you. Thank you. Gracias. Thank you. You are all too kind." More cheers and applause. Carbonero waited. "Gracias. So nice of you to be here on my special day. Thank you. My story is not unique. I am just one of many who owes their baseball prowess to United States El Presidente Numero Cuarenta y cinco." Cheers were followed by large choruses of boos. Carbonero resumed. "It is hard to believe, but so many decades have come and gone since that border wall came crashing down. That..." Carbonero was interrupted by a five-minute standing ovation. When everyone settled back into their seats, Carbonero continued. "...That some of you might not remember, but when that wall was built, it was the best thing for Mexican youth and baseball. At one time the wall stretched for miles. Its intent was to divide. But it failed miserably." Another standing ovation. "Baseball fields sprouted up quicker than weeds all across Mexico and the wall served as the outfield wall for all of those fields. It was wonderful. Our Mexican youth found a new purpose in sports, especially baseball. Not only that, young men from all over the world, including American players, flocked to gain entry into Mexico to play on our pristine fields. Local businesses advertised on the wall. The Mexican economy thrived. And, we owe it all to what's his name's wall! Today, there are more Mexican-born baseball players playing in the major leagues and professionally around the world than any other nationality. Across the way," Carbonero pointed toward the Hall of Fame Museum, "there are pieces of that once standing wall on display. I urge each and everyone one of you to stop in there and to take a look. We must never forget. Oh, and as a little side note, it cost the poor American taxpayers a pretty peso!" Laughter and another standing ovation. Carbonero raised his hands to silence the crowd. "Once upon a time there was a wall. Then came baseball. The wall is long gone as is the forgettable El Presidnete Numero Cuarenta y cinco. Baseball lives. Viva el béisbol!!!"

Green, white and red confetti filled the air. Commissioner Sullivan returned to the fore, shook hands and embraced Carbonero. He had a few prepared closing comments, but thought better of it. The crowd was as interested in hearing him speak as they were in seeing another wall erected.

JACOBO GETS THE GOOD JOB
Phillip Bannowsky

I spent the first two weeks disjointing wings: Among a hundred helmeted and
plastic-aproned associates—they called us—arranged in files either side of several
ringing chicken disassembly lines,
    I would crimp my right wrist up to grip the slimy knife handle with the
most delicate muscles of my thumb and middle finger, then, with index atop the
blade, I'd stab through the shoulder while yanking the wing down with my other
hand, flip the neck back with the blade, and rotate the bird on its conical pedestal
to slice and yank the other wing.
    Next down the line, others made the final cuts to render the wings pretty
much the way they look before they're dredged, deep-fried, saturated in gory
sauce, and served up to beach bums, who never give my aching finger joints and
wrists a second thought.
    Each morning I awoke with fingers swollen stiff, every point of rotation
locked like the dried-out water wheel back home in Peguche. At the last station on
this line was the good job. No knives.
By the time the bird got there, there were the breasts, glistening gray-pink mounds
in pimpled yellow sacs, already cut loose and dangling by a thread of sinew or skin;
All it took was a little tug and they dropped to the white conveyer.

    Tug, drop, tug, drop.

    That's for me. I told the foreman that Friday morning, and he said, "OK."
This was the life. Half the work, twice the time to breathe.
No more worrying when I'd get my yank and slice backwards and stab that blade
into my thumb joint and before I'd felt it, drive clean through, spoiling a whole
line of chickens with pulsing spurts of blood.
    I'd found my home in the American food chain, and as I continued tugging
and dropping I began to contemplate the mechanized wonder of automated chicken
catchers, controlled atmosphere stunning, conveyer chains with chickens in
shackles, plucking machines, and systematic dismembering and packaging for the
market in a miracle of efficiently distributed labor, except for my job, which was
easy and left me half the time to day-dream. The only annoyance was a negligible
twinge beneath my forearm.
    After lunch the rhythm became intoxicating and I had a vision like a sort
of mandala that monks make with colored sand: Golden streams spread from the
spark of creation out to a web of stardust evolving into elements and galaxies, blue
and magenta, spinning planets with drifting continents, braided rivers, and living
beings microbial to mammal, trade routes of sailors, escape routes, and after an
hour that negligible twinge had turned to an intensifying burn driven farther up
both forearms with each tug and drop, but I kept my head in the mandala where

my co-workers from Mexico and Guatemala traveled atop rail cars, through deserts, or packed in U-Hauls along Interstate 5, while overhead were migration paths of flying birds that divided into species that cluck and scratch the ground and get gathered up by chicken catchers from Ecuador and served up to beach bums watching football or *futbol* on television networks broadcasting through transoceanic cables and satellite signals and breaking for ads to sell Coca-Cola or *cerveza* or chicken wings I began to wish I was still cutting because that intensifying burn in my forearms had turned into fiery veins of lava from thumbnails to elbows and the pain sweat was spreading salt in my eyes and a screaming wind was blowing my mandala away and it was a woman crying "*¡Mi hija! Mi hija!*" and the foreman said, "Immigration is here; there is nothing we can do."

"*¡Nuestra Señora!*"

The wing disjointer who had my old job and wing cutter next to him bolted past me and I bolted in their wake, up the stairs to the bathroom, past the bird bath wash-up, through the door to the AC unit and out onto the sun glaring roof where we hid in shadows behind giant aluminum chimneys and vents, ripped off our slimy aprons and helmets, and like commandos peeking out and signaling ran to the next vent and the next and raced all-out for the edge of the roof where my comrades leapt into space and I followed, landing still running on a trailer, and in the field below were ICE agents with flak jackets and rifles. Beyond was a chain link fence with a corner bent back and a dark wood. Off the trailer we landed and rolled to our feet as the ICE agents closed in grabbing first the cutter, and then near the fence the wing disjointer, and I dove through the bent back corner and snagged a belt-loop, but as with the chicken breasts, one tug set me free.

I tunneled through the thick underbrush at the edge of the wood, sprang up under some taller trees, and kicking through fallen twigs like someone wading through the shallows, ran on until my lungs were burning, but not my forearm, and seeing the sunlight cracking through branches I burst out into a cornfield, turned sharply down a long row where I was lacerated by a gauntlet of leaves and finally came upon a small clearing where someone had planted a merry patch of marijuana and there waiting for me was an old black man who carried a machete and said "*Amigo,* do you speak English?"

BLUNDERLAND
Joel & Valerie Reeves

"Mr. Stinger, how will you solve the immigration problem?"

Rex Stinger gazed across the stage at the moderator and realized at once that he was looking into the eyes of the enemy. The liberal media was filled with liars, master inventors of fake news designed to destroy him and his vision of returning America to her former glory. Fortunately, he was so much smarter than all of those television reporters. A lifetime of negotiating real estate deals had prepared him for the role of President in a way no one could even begin to imagine.

Stinger leaned forward on the podium, delighted.

"I will build a great wall," he announced. "And nobody does walls better than me. Very inexpensively. I will build a great, great wall on our southern border and I will have Mexico pay for that wall. Mark my words."

The moderator sat up straighter, eyebrows knitted. "Okay, and how are you—"

"I've got the perfect plan to save this country from the disaster it's becoming," Stinger interrupted. "First of all, we need to trump up national security. We'll have police drones on every street corner with video screens that record every movement. This way, if someone tries to cross the border illegally we'll catch them before they do it."

One of Stinger's supporters in the audience stood, shouting. "Deport the Mexicans! Kick out the Muslims! Bring America back to its former glory!"

A journalist focused his camera on Stinger's supporter, perplexed. The man shoved the camera aside and rushed up toward the stage at Stinger's opponent, Will Hope—an old, slightly hunched man wearing a yamaka. The Stinger supporter pulled out a syringe, pointing it at Hope. The old man backed away, afraid.

"Hey blood-sucking Christ-killer!" the Stinger supporter snarled. "Hope this acid doesn't hit you right in your big nose!"

A spray of liquid burst from the end of the syringe. Stinger, trying to get a swing at a reporter, stepped right into the line of fire. He screamed and covered his face, stumbling forward to the front of the stage. He fell and struck his head hard against the floor, letting out a loud groan just before slipping into unconsciousness. The crowd closed in around him, the auditorium erupting in chaos.

A figure with white gauze wrapped tightly around his face sat on a hospital bed. The doctor stood next to the bed and began gently unwrapping the strips of cloth, talking gently.

"Well, the good news is despite your coma, you still won the presidency!" the doctor announced. "However, the acid left you with some pretty bad scars, so we had to completely redo your face. Your campaign manager assured us that's what you would have wanted."

The doctor stood holding a mirror, studying Stinger.

"Here," he said. "Tell me what you think. I hope you approve. It's the best we could do given none of the faces matched your skin-tone. They must be dead before we take the face, you know."

Stinger rolled his eyes, impatient. "I'm sure it's fine! Just shut up and let me see."

"Well…here it goes," the doctor replied.

Stinger snatched the mirror from the doctor's hands and gazed into it. He screamed, staring at his reflection. Stinger's new face, that of a very attractive Latino, stared back at him: glossy, thick black hair, perfectly unblemished skin, and shiny black eyes.

"Oh, my God!" Stinger ranted. "What have you done? My beautiful face is ruined. I'm disgusting!"

The doctor took a step back. "After your 'Americans Only' law was passed, we've had an overabundance of minority bodies," he explained. "The cemeteries are full. Crematoriums are running full time. One body is gone and five more pop up. Not even scientists have a use for them anymore. The only logical thing to do would be to use one."

Stinger leaped from the bed and shoved his finger in the doctor's face, furious.

"You quack!" he raged. "You're a disgrace to your profession. I'll sue you for malpractice. Change me back now or I'll see you in court."

The doctor shrugged, confident. "I gave you the face of a handsome twenty-five-year-old. Most people would die for such a face. If you take me to court, you will lose."

Stinger glared at him, a bead of spit forming in the corner of his mouth. He shoved the doctor out of the way and stormed out the door.

"Screw you, old man!" he shouted. "I don't need your help! I can get the goddamn face off myself!"

The doctor watched him leave. "Good luck with that."

Stinger slammed the door shut. The doctor picked up the mirror and gazed into it, chuckling to himself.

"Should I tell? Or should I dare? If he goes out, he should beware. Those laws you made, Mr. Stinger, will not take kindly to a man with a Latino face."

He walked over to the window and gazed down at a mean street below, watching as Stinger, his head lowered, walked quickly away.

Stinger stared up at a dull gray foreboding sky filled with blimps displaying his own towering image, face twisted in contempt, his finger pointing menacingly. An electronic billboard along the street also trumpeted Stinger's campaign slogan: "You're either for me or against a strong America."

Everywhere he looked, towering electronic wanted posters scrolled down the sides of buildings. The image of the "criminal" changed from a Muslim to an Asian to a Black to a Latino, the writing underneath reading, "They will bring down America! Capture them dead or alive and receive a special award!"

Inside shop windows, more electronic advertisements displayed homosexual and transsexuals with a caption reading, "Disgusting! Save our children from these heinous acts and receive a special award!"

In the streets, piles of books burned in huge bonfires, along with magazines and bundles of newspapers. Stinger paused, watching as a copy of *To Kill a Mockingbird* was tossed into the flames. He smiled, trembling with pride.

"The world is perfect!" he gloated. "They're using all my good ideas!"

A tattered newspaper blew off the pile of debris, landing at Stinger's feet. He picked it up, the headline reading: *No hope for Hope among Stinger supporters.*

Below the headline was a black and white photo of Will Hope being beaten by Stinger supporters. Stinger chuckled to himself, amused.

"Cool!" he boasted. "I love the press! Wonder what else is in here?"

He flipped to the sports page where he found an article about an event called the Purity Fair. A picture displayed a stereotypical Black and Native American merrily playing carnival games. The caption below the picture read: "Safely observe the humanoids in their natural habitat."

Stinger smiled, his eye drawn to a large, colorful ad:

> *Come and watch Gary the Great perform his magnificent Muslim-taming act! Watch a Latino jump through a hoop of fire! See Blacks form a human pyramid while standing on a ball! Gasp in awe as Asians perform never-before-seen unicycle stunts high above the Big Top without nets! Even get a photo shoot with an LGBT of your choice! Just come on down to the Purity Fair for a night of family fun suitable for all ages!*

Excited, Stinger stuffed the newspaper into his pants pocket. He looked up to see book burners still throwing books onto a bonfire. He rubbed his chin, thinking.

"I wonder if they'd know where the Purity Fair is?" he mused. "You," he shouted. "Burning the books! Do you know where the Purity Fair is? I want to watch it!"

The book burners, a rough-looking group of skinheads sporting plenty of swastikas and nationalistic tattoos, approached him. Getting a better look at Stinger, their faces quickly changed from curiosity to contempt.

"Well, I'll be!" the first burner said, glaring at Stinger. "The Latino wants to watch the Big Top like a pure boy. Sorry, Latino, pures only. *You're* providing the entertainment for the evening."

Stinger stared at him, puzzled, then remembered.

"Wait...what?" he said. "Do you think I'm...?" He laughed. "No! No, I'm not one of *them*! I'm Rex Stinger! I just had some surgery done and this was the only available face! Don't worry, I hate it too! But I'm still me!"

The second burner laughed menacingly. "That's what they all say, you greasy little spic."

The other one made a sudden move toward Stinger. "Let's get him,

George. I hear there's a nice reward for catching them."

Stinger bolted as the two rushed him. He ran faster than he had ever run before down the street and into the alley that led to the subway. He crawled into a train car through the back door and crouched down in the darkness, listening. The lights flickered as he dusted off his shirt and sat down in a passenger seat, breathing heavily.

Stinger glared at the blinking lights, annoyed.

"How pathetic!" he complained. "Not even the lights work correctly on this nightmare on wheels. What? Do they expect me to feed myself, too? What kind of lousy service do they have on these things? God, how do those lazy parasites put up with such crappy hospitality?"

"I know, right?"

Stinger jumped and peered into the darkness. An old man, slightly bent, stepped out of the shadows. Despite the fact that he was now dressed in a dark business suit and tie instead of a white robe and stethoscope, there was no mistaking the man. It was the doctor from the hospital.

"You!" Stinger snarled. "You did this. I want my old face back. People don't like me now."

"I'm sorry if this hasn't all turned out exactly as you had planned," the doctor said. "I'll tell you what, though, President Stinger. I want to help make things right. Let me take you to a place that is more special than any other in your new world. A place with a treasure beyond even your wildest imagining."

Stinger gazed at the man, elated, then shook the doctor's hand vigorously.

"Yes. Take me to the treasure," he exclaimed. "Thanks so much, Doc. I promise you. I won't ever forget this. I might even give you a place on my cabinet."

"No," the doctor replied. "I'm sure you won't. Now, let's get going."

The train rushed through the tunnel in darkness for several minutes before coming to the end. The two men stepped from the subway and gazed ahead at the landscape beyond. Before them, an ivory wall stretched out of sight into the darkness beyond. A leering skull-faced ivory door stood in the middle. Stinger clapped his hands, delighted.

"Oh!" he boasted in triumph. "It's my wall! It's even better than I imagined! Now everyone who sees this wall will know America the beautiful is for whites only! Better yet, it is made of ivory! Now everyone will know of my great wealth, too, because only wealthy people can afford ivory! Not those sniveling wretches beneath me! Tell me, Doctor! How many elephants did it take to build this wall, eh? How many?"

The doctor smiled to himself. "Oh, this ivory didn't come from elephants."

"Rhinos?" Stinger suggested.

The doctor began walking toward the door. Stinger trembled with enthusiasm as the doctor inserted a key into the portal and opened it. However,

Stinger's face fell to pure disappointment when nothing but forest could be seen on the other side. He turned to the doctor, confused.

"All right, Doc," he said. "Where's my treasure? All I see is a stupid bunch of trees! Cut them down and bring me my treasure! Do it now, Doc! Now!"

The doctor studied Stinger, amused. "I'm afraid you don't understand," he said.

"Those woods are worth far more to you right now than any sort of luxury."

Stinger looked at him, annoyed. "Doc, you're not making any sense! Why would I care at all about some lousy patch of trees? My whole job is basically——"

"Because the only thing that stands between you and death is that forest."

Stinger turned around quickly to lecture the doctor, but stopped suddenly when he saw the shiny black revolver. Shocked, Stinger backed away, nervous.

"Doc... what...what are you...." Stinger stammered.

The doctor smirked. "I'm truly sorry, Mr. President, that it has come to this," he said. "But your supporters pay me very well for what they call 'population control.' Basically, I get to go hunting in this forest for those who you may call 'minorities' that either escaped and were captured or were discarded from the Purity Fair. It's not a bad job, really. Keeps me in good shape. But I'm sorry, I can't let one escape, not even you. I must do my 'duty to the State,' you know!"

The blood drained from Stinger's face. "You...you can't be serious! You know who I am. I'm not a minority. I'm Rex Stinger. I'm the President!"

The doctor eyed him coldly, an evil glint in his eyes. "I'll tell you what," he said. "I'll give you a fifteen-minute head start. That's more than the rest got, sir. After all, a President deserves the best, right?"

Stinger's eyes grew wide as the doctor cocked his gun.

"You better start running," the doctor advised. "I'll be coming for you in fifteen."

Stinger stared at the doctor, horrified. The doctor began to raise the weapon. Stinger ran, faster even than he had run before, disappearing quickly into the wilderness. As he ran, Stinger passed the bodies of various minorities sprawled across the ground or hanging from trees. He dodged the corpses as he plunged ahead, gasping.

A blimp passed overhead, the sound of Stinger's own voice broadcast from one of his rallies echoing through the forest. Stinger sprinted ahead, tripping over a dead body in the undergrowth and stumbling forward, the sound of his voice pounding in his ears with each step taken.

The words were clear. The message he had written himself and delivered to a packed auditorium.

"When Mexico sends its people, they're not sending their best. They're not sending you, they're not sending you! They're sending people with problems, and they're bringing their problems. They're bringing drugs, they're bringing crime..."

Stinger tripped over the corpse of a Latino woman and fell to the ground. He looked up to see the doctor standing over him.

"They're rapists…"

Stinger began crying as the doctor pointed the gun at him.

"But some of them are good people, I suppose."

And pulled the trigger.

FIRST PITCH
Kenneth Nichols

Skip told us about Trump a couple days ago. We are in the clubhouse after BP and he sips his cup of coffee and shouts to get our attention. "Guys," he says. "Listen up. I've been informed that our president is going to throw out the first pitch on Opening Day. I know it's a touchy subject. I won't force anyone to catch for him, so if anyone wants to volunteer, let me know before I have to tell the front office."

Most of the guys laugh, some of the white guys pretended they are distracted and rearrange the gear in their lockers. The utility guy beside me from Venezuela scoffs and calls Trump a *becerro*. One of the back-of-the-bullpen guys says in melodious Spanish that Trump's mother's vagina is more stretched out and smells worse than a pair of socks worn every day for a year.

I raise my hand. "I'll do it."

Skip looks at me like I just asked to be sent down to extended Spring Training. "You sure?"

I nod and head back to my locker. Carlos is from Columbia. The first baseball bat he ever held was a broomstick wrapped with duct tape. Now he's one of the best hitters in the world and he makes more money in a year than his father would have made in a hundred lifetimes. "What are you doing, man?" he asks. "That *careverga* wants us both out of the country. Let him throw the ball to himself."

"*Mi amigo,* baseball wasn't the real reason we came to the country. We came because we wanted opportunity. Freedom. I will catch Trump's first pitch because it gives me the chance to do something I never could have done before I left Cuba: to tell *El Presidente* to his face that he has a great opportunity. He has the power to unite everyone who loves the American ideals of independence, hard work and liberty. But he must first understand that he is dividing us. We may speak different languages, we may have grown up with different foods, we may enjoy different kinds of music, but these differences mean so little compared to our shared humanity."

Carlos doesn't know how to respond. He holds out his massive palms, callused from so many swings of the bat and says, "It's your life."

The team kept the arrangement under wraps until the last possible moment. Announcing that a Cuban defector was going to shake Trump's hand and return the baseball would cause unnecessary anger and stress. It was a smart decision. The boos begin when I'm standing at the backstop. President Trump stands at the dugout step, two Secret Service agents in tow. The shouts only get uglier when the announcer's voice booms from the PA: "Ladies and gentlemen. In 1910, President William Howard Taft kicked off the baseball season by throwing out the first pitch in old National Park. Here to continue that tradition, please welcome President Donald J. Trump."

He steps onto our field, waving the bright white baseball through the air as he greets his fellow citizens. I see beer splash from the mouth of a bottle that hits the outfield grass. The man closest to me on the other side of the protective netting screams something he surely wouldn't normally want the little girl beside him to hear. A man in a "Love Trumps Hate" shirt asks in disbelief, "You're going to catch the ball?"

I ignore him and jog out to home plate. Trump has been told the same thing as every other person who throws out a ceremonial first pitch.

You don't have to stand on the mound.

Don't worry about throwing a blistering fastball.

Just get the ball over the plate and the catcher will do the rest.

Trump finishes saluting the crowd and stares in at me. He's ignoring all of the advice. He's standing on the mound, toeing the rubber. There's a fire in his eyes, the same concentration and focus I see when I'm in the batter's box. It's clear he makes my palm sting.

There are many people jeering, a few cheering and the combined sound reaches a crescendo, bouncing between the stadium walls. Trump goes into a little windup, like he's pitching out of the stretch. The pitch is neither the worst nor the best that I have seen. I catch the ball easily and jog out to meet him in the infield. He takes the ball and shakes my hand.

There are 55,000 people in the stadium. More than 300 million in the country. More than 7 billion in the world. At this moment, I and I alone have the attention of the most powerful man on Earth.

"Mr. President, I came to this country because I wanted opportunity. Freedom. I love this country because I have the right to tell you of all people where you have gone astray. I did not have such a gift in my country of birth. You have the power to bring everyone together. All of us, including my fellow immigrants, love the American ideals of independence, hard work and liberty. What are the differences between us? The spices we remember from our childhood? The rhythm of the music that makes us want to dance? The language our mother used to tell us that we are loved? Please bear all of this in mind as you make decisions that affect us all."

The season is now more than a week old. I am told that my jersey sales have plummeted. The president's policies have not changed--how could they in only a week? --and everyone who was scared on Opening Day is still afraid.

What I said jarred him. Before my time with Trump ended and he walked through the tunnel to the clubhouse and I remained in the dugout, I could tell from the way he looked at me that he had heard what I said. My words had touched his soul. Time will tell if the fingerprints I left will remain.

SHAYES' TAXI SERVICE
Steve Smith

Norm Shayes, a fellow Texas Western College student, was parked at a light on a south El Paso street one weekday afternoon when the passenger door was yanked open and a knife-wielding Mexican guy about twenty jumped in and closed the door.

"Hey, man," said the guy. "I need to make it to Fabens, okay? So, let's go." He tapped the knife against the dashboard. "C'mon. Chop chop."

Norm glanced at the people crossing the street in front of his car, at the sidewalks on either side streaming with shoppers or people heading home. Apparently, no one noticed anything unusual. He was alone with a crazed Mexican guy with a knife and who knew what homicidal plan festered in his head. He was a fairly good-looking guy, but his eyes danced with the kind of light Norm associated with a cocaine fix.

Though he had no issues with the Latino population that enlivened the streets and shops of El Paso with their spirited energy and rapid-fire conversation, Norm was unavoidably conscious of the hidden racism weaving through West Texas society that was animated by strong feelings of antipathy from both sides. He had been called *gringo* a number of times, but accepted the anger that produced this as justified, since many of his peers referred to Latinos as greasers and wets. Such attitudes were so ingrained as to be almost casual, making it seem an insoluble problem.

Conflicted thus with ambivalence and rather than argue with the knife, Norm sat on his feelings, and when the light changed, rumbled off. Checking the speedometer, the guy said, "Don't break no laws, man. I don' like cops. Understand?"

Norm picked up on the subtext. "Yeah, I get it."

"Good. So, uhh, what do you do, man? You know, for a living."

Norm looked at the guy. He wore a straight face as if this was a genial conversation between two seat mates on a plane. "You're kidnapping me and you wanna make small talk? For the next thirty miles? Come on."

"Why not, as long as we're traveling together." He smiled.

"Jesus," said Norm, shaking his head.

"Hey, good guess. But it's pronounced Hay'-soos. And your name is . . .?

Norm shook his head. "Forget it."

"Forget it. Is that some kinda Indian name? Like Old Leather Tongue, or Prancing Elk or something." He gazed at Norm. "Come on, don't be a bad sport. As long as we're ridin' along why not get to know each other?"

"You want me to pretend I'm enjoying this? Like we're having a good time?"

"Well, you might as well. I mean you never know when time runs out on you. And there you are going to your reward with a scowl on your face cause you lost the art of enjoying the moment, hey? Personally, I feel that you have to embrace whatever comes your way because what's the alternative? Enjoy the moment I always say. I mean how many do you get? That's the thing. It could be all over in a—"

He stiffened and yelled, "My god, look out!"

Norm froze at the wheel, then saw nothing alarming coming his way. He sagged with relief.

"There now, see what I mean? It could have been a semi barrelin' down on us, and then it's all over."

Norm growled and swung his head in disbelief. "You are crazy."

The guy thought about this. "Nahh, you're just embarrassed to consider that I might be right. That my jumpin' in your car just could be the lesson you need to set your life on the right path. To put yourself right with the, the universe. Let me tell you, when you get home you're gonna be refreshed in mind and spirit, all because some guy you didn't even know forced you out of your, what do they call it—you, know, when you're stuck in a rut and are just going through the motions—complacency, that's it. Complacency. That's when you need your outlook changed. And that's why I'm here." He smiled. "My name ain't Jesus for nothing."

"Blessed be thy name," said Norm.

"All the same, I feel I've done something for the good of mankind. I've paid back my rude interruption into your complacent life. You should thank me. In a way, it's been a kind of sacrifice on my part, you know."

Norm laughed humorlessly. "You're absolutely right. I owe you an apology along with my pitiful, shabby thanks for not welcoming you into my car. What's my gas money and wear and tear on my car and the fright you gave me with your damn knife compared to your holy mission of saving others from themselves. You deserve a halo."

The guy laughed. Norm shrugged and gave up. thirty-minutes later they drove in the city limits of Fabens. At the beginning of the business district, the guy said, "This is good. Pull over."

Norm eased to the curb and shifted to park. The guy got out.

"Hey, thanks man," he said smiling. "You're all right. I could grow to like you if you weren't so damn white." He fumbled in his shirt pocket. "Nuts, I'm out of business cards, so I guess we'll probably never run into each other again . . . unless—listen, we're having a big family get together next weekend if you'd like to come?"

Norm studied him and felt a wry, unbelieving grin break across his face. Shaking his head, he said, "Why not. So, what's your last name. Next time I'm in Fabens, the manure capital of West Texas, I'll give you a ring and see if you need a lift anywhere."

The guy gazed at Norm and laughed. Then he closed the door and walked down a nearby alley. As it was late, and Norm had another day of finals coming up, he drove back to El Paso. Along the way he caught himself laughing from time to time, without humor. Once he got home he phoned the incident in to the police.

The write-up appeared in the El Paso Times the next morning under the heading: "Local Man Car-jacked and Forced to Carry Knife-wielding Passenger to Fabens."

I read the story the next morning at breakfast. I knew Norm from high school for being excitable and a touch paranoid and, imagining his shaky reaction, had to laugh.

I boarded my neighborhood bus to downtown El Paso intending to transfer to the bus to Texas Western. While waiting in front of downtown El Paso's YMCA building, I realized that my bus had run late and I had missed my usual connection to the college some three miles north of the city center. I was going to be ten minutes late for an important final exam.

Sitting on the Y's concrete steps by the bus stop, I grew tense and began rocking from side to side in agitation. If I missed the final I'd lose three important class credits toward my bachelor's degree in journalism. I said some words I wouldn't want my mom to hear. I began watching for a passing taxi.

Just then a car bearing a TWC parking permit in the upper right of the windshield drove up and stopped at the light. The word Hallelujah strobed my antic mind with Day-Glo vividness. On impulse I jumped up, dashed to the car, yanked the door open and jumped in.

Uttering a cry of terror, the driver lunged against his window with his hands held in front of his chest. Then he recognized me and sagged in relief. Dumping a massive sigh, he said, "Jesus Christ, Smith, you almost stopped my heart." He studied me with a mixture of fear and anger still distorting his features, then pronounced, "You asshole." He blew out some tension through puffed cheeks and shook his head slowly.

"Sorry, Norm," I said. "But I'm desperate. Got a final and can't be late. But you know, you really ought to keep your doors locked. Anybody could jump in and force you to take him wherever they wanted to go."

Norm stared at me without blinking. I gazed back. "Uhh, It's gettin' kinda late, man. Could you . . . you know, get moving?"

Norm bared most of his teeth, but not in a smile. He yanked the gearshift into first and gunned it. "You know, Smith," he said with a touch of scorn, "I think I liked the Mexican guy better. At least he didn't give me a phony lecture. The more I think about it, I liked him a whole lot better."

He was quiet for a time, then muttered, "Jerk."

"Yeah, man, I deserve that. I'm sorry. It was just a crummy coincidence." Five minutes later I asked, "Did the guy threaten you?"

"Whattaya think, bozo! He had a damn knife."

"Yeah, that would do it for me, allright." And this opened Norm up. I listened sympathetically as he spilled the whole story out in what felt to me like a catharsis, trying not to show the humor I was feeling at the Mexican guy's sardonic sense of humor and brazen way of working out his travel needs. When Norm finished he turned a look on me and made me promise not to share the story with anyone, "I mean anyone!"

I agreed. But that night I wrote it down in story form from memory. When I turned it into my evening writing class prof a week later, I got a B. My prof, who was the faculty advisor for the monthly college journal, *The Desert Speaks*—which featured the writing of students in the MFA program—wanted to include it in the next issue, but the vision of Norm Shayes slapping my downy cheeks with a leather glove and coldly saying "Pick your weapon," decided the issue for me.

LEAVE IT TO BEAVER
Tyson West

"Guys, when you said we were going to the Museum of the Revolution, I figured there would be some drinking done," Darnell groaned, after he parked his father's car on a not so clean back street of Saltillo, Mexico, "but this is a whorehouse." When Johnny and Javier, two popular football players, invited him on a road trip to Mexico, he figured he would be their designated driver, but not designated pimp.

Johnny, 250 pounds of fast blond muscle, was grateful that Darnell sweet talked the cop into overlooking the half case of Coronas on their last trip. They lost the beer, but he kept his eligibility.

Javier wheedled, "We'll get there, Beaver. Let's have a little side trip first. Jack and Butch had a much better time with the girls here than with the cheerleaders back home."

Darnell didn't care what Johnny and Javier did, but his girlfriend, Leslie, might learn he had been here. Granted he and Leslie had only gone as far as some heavy petting, but he felt he should care.

"Can I just stay in the car?"

"Remember we agreed not to get separated. We could get kidnapped."

"Kidnapped? You said that stuff like that didn't happen here 150 miles south of the border."

"A couple of Americans got kidnapped here last week. You speak really good Spanish. You've already proven you can talk us out of anything, but it's best you come in. You can listen to the piano player."

Johnny giggled, "They may charge you a cover charge whether you munch on anything or not. You might as well get the full meal deal if you have to pay just to get in."

Javier turned to Johnny, "No. I'm sure we can talk them into not charging if he just warms the bench."

"I'll text Leslie and tell her how nice the museum is." Darnell groused as he took his thick glasses off to clean.

"That's the spirit, Beaver."

Johnny knocked softly. The door opened a crack and two dark slightly crossed eyes locked on Darnell. With a flattened forehead, the wiry young girl, a couple inches over five feet seemed exotic, but not terribly sexy.

Javier nudged Darnell. "Tell her that we spoke to Pablo in Monterey at the Toro Bravo. He said to ask for Pilar."

After Darnell translated, she replied in a strangely accented Spanish. "I will talk to Pilar."

A few minutes later, a tall woman in her forties with braided black hair wearing a long red velvet dress appeared. "What can I do for you gentlemen?"

"Is it possible for us to enjoy the company of ladies here?"

51

"There may be ladies here interested in visiting with you. Come in."

Johnny and Javier led the way. Darnell followed reluctantly. Darnell looked more carefully at the girl who had answered the door. Her simple white shift dress set off her strong brown legs and arms. He saw her profile now. She had a curved nose and thick lips.

He spoke to Pilar softly. "That girl who answered the door, she's not Mexican, is she?"

"No. She's an Indian from El Salvador."

Darnell could not take his eyes off of her. She looked like a carving on a Mayan temple come to life.

They were led into a large parlor with a piano in the corner, but no piano player. The sound system played Flaco Jimenez and narco corridos. Along a wall a thin dark man stood behind a bar. "Seniors, would you like drinks?"

Johnny spoke up, "Margaritas con Hornitos tequila."

Darnell grinned. Johnny, a very poor Spanish student, could flawlessly order a drink. Javier ordered a tequila sunrise in perfect Spanish. Darnell mumbled, "Jarritos."

"Que tipo?

"Tutifruti."

The bar tender grinned, "No tiene, pero tango guayaba."

"Bien."

As he picked up his soft drink, Darnell noticed that the girl who answered the door was staring at him.

Pilar had called the other girls down. They lined up and smiled at the boys.

A tall girl with dyed blond hair and a full figure was talking to another girl in the corner and giggling. Another lean girl with long black hair sat and watched quietly chewing gum.

Pilar asked softly, "Who would you like to spend some time with?"

Johnny pointed to the tall blond.

Javier picked out a thinner smiling girl with a bobbed haircut and dark almond eyes.

"Y tu, Darnell?"

"Nada."

Pilar immediately fired at him in rapid Spanish, "What do you mean none of them? My girls are offended that you would not find one of them desirable."

"But, I have a girlfriend back home. She might be offended." He fired back.

All the girls looked away from him. Some whispered to one another. A couple giggled.

"I'm sorry," Pilar said. "You will have to spend some time with one of these ladies. What you do with her is between the two of you. But I will not let you hurt the feelings of my girls that you find none of them desirable."

Darnell turned to the girl who answered the door. As she wore unskillfully applied makeup and had fine hair on her legs, he hoped she was a servant with whom he could just talk.

However, before he could speak, she strode up to him and took his hand. She smiled at Pilar, "He asked me."

Pilar was surprised. "Michelle, I've never seen you so forward."

"His soul needs me."

"Is this the woman you want?"

Darnell felt overwhelmed with a desire to protect Michelle and her feelings, "Yes."

Darnell could almost read Johnny and Javier's minds. "With all these good looking chicas, he picks the ugliest."

He didn't care about what they might say on a drinking session with their teammates. It felt right to be with her. They could just talk. He began to feel his concern about what Leslie may think becoming untethered.

Johnny and Javier bought drinks for their girls. Darnell asked Michelle if she wanted one.

"Si." She ordered a lemon and lime Jarritos.

They sat at a table. Michelle crossed her legs, "They call me Michelle but *you* can call me by my Indian name, Ix Chel, the jaguar goddess."

Although Spanish was not her first language nor was it Darnell's, they soon found they could speak with their eyes, gestures and smiles.

"I don't want to offend you. You are very beautiful. But I just want to talk."

"We have a lot to talk about."

Johnny and Javier took their girls upstairs. Darnell kept looking into Ix Chel eyes until she spoke.

"We should go upstairs now to talk."

After they entered their room, Darnell sat in a chair while Ix Chel lay on the bed. "I would like us to lie on the bed," Ix Chel whispered. "I want to put the bed down as if we had made love. If Pilar does not think that you are satisfied, it will go hard on me."

"How did you get here?"

"I was sold and bought. A gang was after my brother. We decided to run north together to the United States. If he left and I stayed and a rival gang caught me, there's no telling what they may do.

"There is another reason I can't go home. I'm a bruja."

"You a witch? Why do they say that?"

"Because I have a third nipple. When something happened in our home town, a sudden death or a violent tropical storm, villagers whispered it is my doing. My brother and I were separated. I don't know if he's alive."

"Do many men choose you?"

"None. I use my spells to keep them away."

"Then why do they keep you here?"

"Because I clean and serve Pilar. You're the only man that wanted me."

"You're the most beautiful here."

"That you can see that tells me you are special. It's best if you put your arms around me. We don't need to do anything. Just hold me. It would make me feel safe."

As Darnell put his arms around Ix Chel, she leaned her head on his shoulder.

"I dream about escaping. How did your family reach the United States?"

"My great grandfather and great grandmother were born in the old country in Germany and Poland."

"Why did they leave?"

"Great grandfather did not want to get drafted into the Russian army. Poland was part of Russia then. When the Czar was looking for a few good men, soldiers went to villages to take the older boys. He fled into Germany. My great grandmother's father was a violent drunk and her life was hell. She lied about her age. They married and caught a steamship out of Hamburg to Ellis Island."

"Your great grandfather saved her?"

"That's what family lore says."

"How old was he when this happened."

"As old as I am now."

Suddenly she closed her eyes and fell into a trance clinging to Darnell. He froze not knowing what to do. He shook her but she did not respond. Then after ten minutes she abruptly whispered, "Thank you." Her eyes opened. "Your friends are bigger, but I see now you're more powerful. You are my destiny."

Darnell was shocked. "What would Leslie say?" he thought, "It didn't matter. Leslie did not need him. Besides he wasn't marrying Ix Chel, merely saving her from hell." Something in him locked — something he had never felt before. He felt needed and powerful as if an angel was guarding him — no — he had become the angel.

Darnell whispered, "I'll get you north. It will not be easy. I don't know anything about the immigration laws. I can say you are my wife."

She rolled over on top of him and put her arms tightly around him and buried her head in his shoulder next to his.

"I can find my own place when I get there, but only you can save me."

Part of Darnell knew she sounded corny, and that what he was about to do was crazier than anything they had ever done. Now he was going to get Johnny and Javier into something. He was determined to smuggle Ix Chel across the border.

He opened his eyes and looked into hers. It was kind of sexy the way her dark eyes were crossed, but he wanted no sex with her unless he earned it. Saving Ix Chel was a greater high than any orgasm.

He spoke, surprised at his cool calculation. "If we can get a fake Texas driver's license and US passport made for you, we can cross together. We can swim the river or climb over the border wall. If they catch us and we have wedding rings it will seem real."

"If we have fake papers it makes more sense to cross in the car as if we are coming home from a trip," she whispered into his ear.

"Yes, that would make the most sense." He nodded then kissed her. "When my friends leave they will want to eat and drink. Do you know a restaurant?"

"Yes. Barillas on the Calle del Revolution is across from the Church of San Judas."

"Will you have something to eat?"

"Yes. I'll eat before I go. I'll meet you at the church."

"How will we cross the border?"

"The answers will come to us when we get there."

As they left, Darnell told Pilar how charming a companion Ix Chel had been.

Johnny and Javier grinned and giggled drunkenly as they got in the car.

"All those gorgeous girls, Beaver, and you picked out the ugliest one in the house!"

Darnell laughed back, "The ugly ones have to try harder. Let's eat. She told me where there's a great restaurant."

"As long as they don't run out of tequila, we're fine."

After they left the restaurant, Darnell told the even drunker Johnny and Javier to sit in the car while he checked out the church.

Halfway across the street, Ix Chel materialized beside him.

"Let's go, Cariño . The sooner we get north the less time Pilar will have to find me."

"Should we head to Monterey?"

"Yes. We can get lost there and get fake papers."

"It would be better if you sat behind me as I'm driving. I'd like you to be beside me, but Johnny will draw attention away from you."

"You're so crafty," she kissed him on the cheek.

At the car Darnell introduced her, "I want you to meet Ix Chel."

"What's she doing here?"

"We're taking her back to the United States."

Javier sneered. "Jesus, are you in love or what?"

"I'm helping her. She was sold into slavery. The least I can do is free her."

"Is this going to get us in trouble with the law?" Johnny asked.

"No more than drinking and driving."

"We are not interested in you getting us in trouble."

Darnell looked his companions hard in the eye. "I put up with the shit you two get into and I get you out of. It's my turn now. I get to do the dumbass crazy thing and you guys get to blame me if something goes south. But we will do one better. This time I'm going to get us into trouble and Ix Chel and I will get us out. Shut your mouths."

"We got something to say about this."

"Yeah, and if I pull over and talk to the Federales, and Ix Chel and I tell a tale in Spanish that you can't understand, I wonder which jail they will put you in."

Johnny turned to Darnell. "How do you know she ain't lying to you?"

Darnell got a strange look on his face, "I believe her because I believe in her."

Javier laughed. "I never would have thought you had it in you, Beaver. Why you want step up to the plate for this ugly little puta is beyond me."

"I'm not going to call you out for pistols for two and coffee for one for that comment this time, Buddy. Don't you ever call her ugly again, or I'll have you in a cockroach infested jail with Juan Grande playing 'Quien es mas macho.' We are getting her across the border."

Javier, though drunk and a bit peeved, suddenly sensed the little bruja's power. Darnell would not hesitate to throw him and Johnny into hell to save her. "I sincerely apologize if I offended Ix Chel and you. We will go nowhere without her."

Darnell translated to Ix Chel, "Cariña, he is sorry for his rash words."

She held onto Darnell's arm, "Mi Vida, I feel so safe with you."

After they picked up her false papers, Darnell gently kissed Ix Chel who was now seated next to him with Johnny screening her to the right. As they drove north, Ix Chel and Darnell were already quarreling over which direction to go.

EIGHT DECADES ON
Maverick Smith

I half-expected my father to call begging for shelter, for succor, for sanctuary, once the president had made his announcement that all illegal aliens were to be deported. My father had made it clear before he walked out on me and Mamá that he never wanted to go back to his home country, a land he associated with shattered dreams and crushed hopes. But it was my captain who called instead.

"You saw the news?" Captain Alejandra's usual level voice was flat. It was only through long familiarity that I recognized the dispassionate tone she used when she disliked a directive.

"Yes." I replied. There was a pause on the line.

"I have received word from higher up. I'm calling you back from your leave temporarily."

"What?" I rested one hand on my belly. A small bump was already beginning to show. "Are you certain that I am the best available agent?"

"Yes." Alejandra said firmly. "José Luis and Diego have influenza. Andrès is attending a family event out of town. Detaining people for deportation is a sensitive matter. My boss does not want two junior agents paired together alone."

"I need a physical to ensure I am fit for the field."

"I took the liberty of booking one for you with the professionals you had on file for nine am." Paper rustled in the background. When Alejandra spoke again her voice was hesitant and human. "Do you….if you want to refuse this assignment on personal grounds, tell me. I have the paperwork in my hands. I can fax it to you."

"Personal grounds? You mean my pregnancy?"

"Officially, yes. Unofficially, I mean your biological father."

"Mamá told you?" I sucked in a breath. The protective hand on my belly curled into a fist. "She had no business-"

"She told me that year you brought me home for Revolution Day." Alejandra explained. "You remember, that year we were dating?"

"I remember." I said numbly.

"She was showing me some old photo albums. We came across a picture and I asked her about it. I don't think she understood the implications of you being in law enforcement when she told me."

"She grew up in the era of the drug wars." I reminded her. "As far as I know, she still tells the neighbors I shuffle papers all day to protect me."

"Still, she told me she was proud that her daughter was a member of the federales." Alejandra lowered her voice. "She said was proud of both of us. She used that American expression…called us a 'power couple.'"

"I should go." I said quickly and listed off several excuses at random. I did not want to talk about our relationship or rehash how it had ended.

"You have no personal problem implementing the presidential directive, then?" Alejandra offered me one last effort to decline. I swore I detected a hint of pleading in Alejandra's voice.

"Like you said, I am a member of the federales. Obeying orders is what I do."

"Come back in a week." Esmerelda told me as she stripped off her disposable gloves. The appointment had taken an hour but me and the baby were fine. "If you are running around rounding up fugitives, it is important you have regular check-ups to ensure we catch any complications early."

Fugitives, Esmerelda said. I thought of my father, a tall soft-spoken man who had taught me how to read using song lyrics from his homeland. It was easier to remember Mamá quarrelling with him because this choice of teaching material had included the colonist anthem *This Land is My Land* than it was to bring his fuzzy features into focus. I certainly didn't see his half-remembered features among those of the pale, gun-toting U.S.A border bandits Alejandra had tacked to the board when I walked into work. She paused the pep talk she was giving the junior agents.

"Here." She pushed a government brochure into my unresisting hands and resumed talking. The brochure was entitled 'Ten Take-downs for Illegal Aliens.' I skimmed it while she resumed her speech.

"…do not be mistaken. These people will not like you for sending them home. They will use bribery, beseeching and begging to make you disregard your orders. They will wail about the horrors of the U.S.A, calling it a corrupt nation full of nasty politicians where rape and murder are a normal as sunrise and sunset. These are lies."

Alejandra slammed her open palm on the nearest desk as she spoke the last word. The junior agents flinched at the resulting metallic bang.

"You will be working as trio on this one. As the more senior agent, Itzel will take point. Any questions?"

She swept the room with her gaze. It was a rhetorical question mood but one of the new agents raised a timid hand.

"Sir? I don't understand the politics here. Didn't these illegal aliens elect the very leaders they fled the U.S.A to escape? Why didn't they just un-elect then instead of jumping the border?"

Because our politicians are crooked as the day is long, the illegals who hung out at the bar in Mamá's village would have said. I said nothing and made a pretense of being engrossed in the propaganda I was reading while my vision blurred with tears. Fracking pregnancy hormones.

"And I don't understand these age ranges, sir." The other junior agent chimed in when Alejandra did not answer immediately. "Why is it important for national security that we deport a seventy-year old individual? Their families and their lives are on this side of the border not in that barren desert to the north."

"The politics of this situation are not our problem." Alejandra said coldly. "We swore an oath to follow the orders we have been given."

"Sir, yes, sir." I joined in the group salute but let the junior agents proceed me to the equipment room. Alejandra's stoic demeanor disintegrated when once the junior agents had turned their backs. She looked small and fragile like the porcelain doll I had gotten from well-meaning relatives at my quinceañera. I stayed behind because I needed to update my captain about the results of my physical not because I wanted to talk to Alejandra one-on-one. At least, that was what I told myself.

"Come back in a week, they said?" Alejandra looked me up and down, her gaze stopping on my belly. "You look fine. You've got that healthy pregnancy glow all the books mentioned. So why a weekly check-up?"

"The doctor and the midwife are being cautious." I explained patiently while a part of my mind marveled that she had been doing research about pregnancies. My desire to have children was what had ended our relationship, after all.

"Cautious?" She still looked confused.

"Most woman in their first trimester aren't kicking down doors and taking names as part of their job." I elaborated, my tone dry as the Great Salt Plain. My father, I remembered, had become very sad when I brought home maps from school that showed just how the Great Salt Plan had spread to cover most the entire U.S.A. I explained I had edged green lines of growing plants at the borders as the teacher had instructed but this had not made him happy. In his memories, the U.S.A had been a green growing with endless fields of food.

Later that school year, I had peppered him with questions about a news broadcast. I wanted to know if a theocracy was like a democracy and why everyone was so worried that the militias in his homeland had arms because everyone had two arms, according to the teacher in my English class. This too, made him sad. He told me his homeland's decline started with the election of an flame-haired, orange-skinned old man. He had promised to explain more when I was older. It was one of the promises he never ended up keeping. Alejandra cleared her throat, bringing me back to the present.

"I will try to get you back on your leave soon. It is an unfortunate coincidence that presently the three other senior agents are unavailable."

"Yes. It is most unfortunate." I answered, unsure if I should tell her of my suspicions. I knew two of the unavailable agents had friends in the immigration office and might have coincidently become ill to avoid detaining people. The third out-of-town agent likely had illegal aliens as friends or family in his provincial hometown that he was using this festival as an excuse to warn them to hide or flee to the highlands. I suddenly sharply glad my father was not in my life.

"I really am sorry about this." Alejandra misunderstood my silence. "Be careful out there, okay? Sticking to arresting grandmothers and leave the gun-toting illegal aliens to the junior agents."

As a joke, it fell flat but I managed a weak smile anyway. My mind whirled with confusion as I made my way to the equipment room. Alejandra had stopped asking me to be careful on the job after we stopped dating, stating that she did not want to be accused of favoritism. I wondered if this baby meant she saw me as more fragile or if was there more than professional courtesy behind her words. I would ask her later, I decided, as I signed out my service weapon. My body amour didn't fit as well as it once did thanks to the baby bump. I made a mental note to have Alejandra order in a larger size for me after this shift. For now, I had to go arrest some illegal aliens.

Our first arrest was a young man with blond peach fuzz on his tanned cheeks. He dropped his construction tools in the dirt and ran into the nearest unfinished building as the three of us strode into the building site. Mindful of Alejandra's words, I had the junior agents go after him while I checked rest of workers' papers. Three carpenters, two plumbers, one journeyman and a handful of electricians later, the agents came back with the illegal alien sandwiched between them.

"Nasty female federales." He spat when he saw me. He was cuffed with twist ties sported a nasty scape on one muscular forearm. His spittle landed near the toe of my boot.

"There is a barbed wire fence at the behind the building." Ana explained when she saw my gaze lingering on it. "He tried to climb it."

I grunted an acknowledgement of her words but once we dropped the young man off at the closest detention center I found it hard to put that wound from my thoughts. Given his dark, dank accommodations and lack of medical care in detention, the wound would probably fester. I found my eyes growing moist again. Fracking pregnancy hormones.

Our next arrest took place in the oddest of settings, a hospital. A matriarch had come into the emergency room after suffering a heart attack. As the nurses bustled around making her comfortable and reassuring her assembled family, the cardiologist had asked for the woman's papers. After much hemming and hawing from the woman's assembled kin, they admitted she had none. So, the hospital had called the federales.

"It was a minor heart attack, you understand." The cardiologist stressed to me as he escorted me toward the woman's room. "So, there is no medical reason she cannot be detained."

"I see." I said as he drew back a drape and I was confronted with the sight of a small shriveled elderly woman who, other than her skin tone, could have been my grandmother. The resemblance made me wipe tears from my traitorous eyes.

"Ma'am?" The doctor sounded concerned. "Is everything okay?"
No. I clamped my lips shut against my automatic response.

"Everything is fine, doctor. Go back to your rounds. We will take over from here." I turned slightly and beckoned for the two junior agents behind me to come into the room. In the split second my attention was not on the room in front of me, the illegal alien struck. I classified him as such based on his shock of blond hair but what really gave it away was the wildness in his eyes as he wielded a shining scalpel.

He must have been hiding behind the bed, I thought as he charged toward me, screaming something about his mother and never going back. I pulled my service weapon from my belt. Memories of training drills flashed through my head, telling me how close he needed to get and where exactly I needed to hit him to achieve the outcome I wanted. It was only after he was sprawled unconscious at my feet with a lump rising on his skull that my brain registered the scalpel sticking out of my belly. I was trying to reassure the junior agents that I was fine and calm the hysterical old woman who was agitated enough that I feared she would have another heart attack when my vision went fuzzy then black.

Someone was holding my hand. That was the first sensation that penetrated my mind. It was rapidly followed by the feel of starched sheets underneath me and the sensation of being enveloped in a billowing poncho that for some reason had armholes and was too short to over me properly. A familiar voice mumbled a prayer beside me in choppy Latin phrases. "Wake up." The voice added in Spanish.

I felt a smile alight upon my lips before my eyes were properly open. Even then, I blinked several times before I took in the improbable sight of my captain, sitting beside the hospital bed dressed in civilian clothes.

"You're here." I said inanely.

"Where else would I be?" She answered. "I certainly wasn't going to stay at the office. My phone has been ringing off the hook since the woman I lo-care about got stabbed in the line of duty. Your Mamá has been demanding updates every half-hour, I'll have you know."

"Well, you can tell her I'm fine." The ridiculous hospital gown ended just above my ankles. The baby bump looked bigger from this horizontal position. "We are fine, right?"

"Yes. You and the baby are fine." Alejandra ran a finger over my knuckles. "You and I are fine, too. Well, better than fine. If you want us to be."

"What do you mean?"

"It took you getting stabbed to make me realize I don't want to lose you. I want you in my life." She paused, worrying her lower lip between her teeth. "I want both of you in my life."

"What about changing nappies and dealing with teething?" I asked, citing two reasons she had been against babies before.

"We will have family and friends to help out with the baby. Besides," Alejandra squared her shoulders like she was preparing to charge into an encampment of illegal aliens. "Nappies and teething are only a very small portion of being a parent. At least that is what the parenting books tell me."

"You know, you researching habit is pretty cute." I smiled at her.

"How cute?" She raised an eyebrow.

"Cute enough for me to ask you to pull that drape across the door." It was rare that I got to order my superior officer around. But she was smiling when she did so.

CONTRIBUTOR BIOS

XANATH CARAZA is a traveler, educator, poet and short story writer. She is a columnist of La Bloga, Smithsonian Latino Center, Periódico de Poesía and Revista Zona de Ocio. Her books are Lágrima roja, Sin preámbulos / Without Preamble, Le sillabe del vento / Sílabas de viento, Donde la luz es violeta / Where the Light is Violet, Tinta negra / Black Ink, Ocelocíhuatl, Sílabas de viento / Syllables of Wind, Noche de colibríes, Corazón pintado, Conjuro, her short story collection, Lo que trae la marea / What the Tide Brings, and her second short story collection, Pulsación, is in progress.

ANDERS CARLSON-WEE is a 2015 NEA Creative Writing Fellow and the author of *Dynamite*, winner of the 2015 Frost Place Chapbook Prize. His work has appeared in *Ploughshares*, *New England Review*, *The Sun*, *AGNI*, *Poetry Daily*, *Best New Poets*, *The Best American Nonrequired Reading*, and *Narrative Magazine*, which also featured him on its "30 Below 30" list of young writers to watch. Winner of *Ninth Letter*'s Poetry Award, *Blue Mesa Review*'s Poetry Prize, and *New Delta Review*'s Editors' Choice Prize, he was runner-up for the 2016 Discovery/*Boston Review* Poetry Prize. With his brother Kai, he is coauthor of two chapbooks: *Mercy Songs* and *Two-Headed Boy*, winner of the 2016 David Blair Memorial Chapbook Prize. His work has been translated into Chinese. He lives in Minneapolis, where he serves as a McKnight Foundation Creative Writing Fellow.

EDWARD VIDAURRE has been published in several anthologies and literary journals among them La Bloga, La Tolteca Zine, Bordersenses, Interstice, La Noria Literary Journal, Boundless Anthology of the Valley International Poetry Festival 2011-2013. He's had four books published - 'I Took My Barrio On A Road Trip' (Slough Press 2013), 'Insomnia' (El Zarape Press 2014), 'Beautiful Scars' (El Zarape Press2015), and 'Chicano Blood Transfusion' (FlowerSong Books, 2016) He also co-edited TWENTY-Poems in Memoriam and Boundless 2014 the Anthology of the Rio Grande Valley International Poetry Festival.

DON MATHIS The life of Don Mathis revolves around the many poetry circles in San Antonio. His poems have been published in several anthologies and periodicals and broadcasted on local TV and national radio. In addition to poetry, he has also written policy and procedures for academia and aviation, case histories for psychological firms, and news and reviews for various media.

PW COVINGTON'S writing is raw, powerful, and carries the voice of his hard-lived curriculum vitae. His poetry and prose is undeniably of Beat lineage, and his words have the power to carry the full weight of desperate yet hopeful experience.

Incarceration, Poverty, War, Heartbreak, Homelessness, Isolation, these are the roots of Covington's work, but his voice is neither bitter nor caustic. It is, in his own way, hopeful.

SERES JAIME MAGAÑA was born in Guadalajara, Jalisco, Mexico. He is a student of literature and a writer. He has published in the Rio Grande Valley International Poetry Festival Boundless Anthology 2015 and 2016, South Texas College Interstice 2015 and 2016, Art Young's Good Morning and Garbanzo Literary Magazine Jan 2017 Issue, the Acentos Review Feb 2017 Issue, and has one self-published book titled 'Seven Blossoms'. He enjoys reading his poetry and short stories around the Rio Grande Valley where he currently lives with his family. For more of his writing check out his page on FaceBook @seresjaimemaganaauthor and to reach him you can email him at seresmaganaauthor@gmail.com

JOSE SANCHEZ Musician (I Ching Gatos), Storyteller, Educator

MÓNICA ALVAREZ is a Mexican writer whose work is committed to social justice, utilizing art as a vessel to share the stories of those who have been overlooked and silenced by the ones in power. She holds a Master's in Spanish Literature and is currently working in obtaining her Master's in Interdisciplinary Studies in Mexican American Studies as well as her MFA in Creative Writing. She has participated in local literary and academic events, such as: Tercer Coloquio Estudiantil sobre lengua, literatura y creación literaria en la frontera, Los Santos Días de la Poesía, XI Congreso Binacional Letras en el Estuario, Espirales al Viento, Festiba, NACCS Tejas Foco, The International Poetry Festival, etc. She is committed to activist work that advocates for the rights and values the cultures of her Community.

BRI IANNIELLO

DEBBIE GUZZI Author of The Hurricane
available at https://www.the-hurricanedg.com/books

FERNANDO ESTEBAN FLORES graduated from the University of
Texas at Austin with a B.A. in English. He taught writing at
several secondary schools in San Antonio and received 2 ExCEL
awards for excellence in teaching from KENS 5-TV, and was
chosen as a distinguished educator from Bexar County by Trinity
University's Trinity Prize Committee. His work has appeared in:
the San Antonio Express-News, Voices de la Luna, The Americas
Review, The Texas Observer, The Thing Itself Journal (Our Lady
of the Lake University), rogueagent journal (issue 25), Written
with a Spoon: a Poet's Cookbook, Is This Forever or What?, Lost
Children of the River, (The Raving Press),
writersoftheriogrande.com and was nominated for a Pushcart Prize
in poetry. His three books of poetry: Ragged Borders, Red
Accordion Blues & BloodSongs are available from Hijo del Sol
Publishing and were recently archived at the Ozuna Learning
Center & Library at Palo Alto College. Visit his webpage:
www.madwarbler.com

STEVEN RAY SMITh's poetry has appeared in Slice, The Yale
Review, Southwest Review, The Kenyon Review, Pembroke
Magazine, Grain, Puerto del Sol and others. Recent work is
published in the The Columbia College Literary Review and The
Suburban Review. New work is forthcoming from The Beechwood
Review and Clarion. A complete list of publications is at
www.StevenRaySmith.org. He was raised on the Texas border and
currently lives in Austin.

ANA M. FORES TAMAYO Being an academic who was not paid
enough for her trouble, Ana M. Fores Tamayo — ABD in
Comparative Literature from New York University— wanted to do
something that really mattered to her, work with asylum seekers.
She began to advocate for marginalized refugee families from
Mexico and Central America, trying to raise awareness of
immigrants who flee their homeland. She writes about these

experiences and thoughts on her blog (http://adjunct-justice.blogspot.com).

Although working with asylum seekers is heart wrenching work, it is at the same time quite satisfying, being able to help others one to one. It is also quite humbling. Her work has helped her with her own sense of displacement, having been a child refugee, always trying to find a new home. In parallel, her poetry has become another side, the hidden side she does not often let others see, although lately, it has been trying to come out into the world.

PRISCILLA CELINA SUAREZ is the 2015-17 McAllen Poet Laureate and has been a recipient of the Mexicasa Writing Fellowship. A RGV native, her poetry is a hybrid of rancheras, polkas, pop, rock, and musica internacional. A past contributor to the American Library Association's YALS magazine, she has also authored the Texas State Library's Bilingual Programs Chapter – allowing her an opportunity to gain experience in writing poetry, rhymes, and tongue twisters for children and teens.
Most recently, Lina released an eBook titled Cuentos Wela Told Me: That Scared the Beeswax Out of Me!. Her poetry was included in ¡Juventud!: Growing up on the Border and Along the River III: Dark Voices from the Río Grande. In 2003, her work was selected by the Monitor staff as 'The Best Poetry of the Year'.

LYNNE S VITI teaches in the Writing Program at Wellesley College She has authored numerous academic articles on legal topics, composition theory and pedagogy, literature and media. Her poetry chapbook, Baltimore Girls, was published in March 2017 by Finishing Line Press. Her poetry, nonfiction and fiction has appeared in over sixty online and print journals and anthologies, including The Wire: Urban Decay and American Television (2009), The Baltimore Sun, Amuse-Bouche, The Paterson Review, The Little Patuxent Review, Drunk Monkeys, Cultured Vultures, Incandescent Mind, and Right Hand Pointing. She won an Honorable Mention in the 2015 Allen Ginsberg Poetry Contest, and the summer 2015 music poetry contest at The Song Is. Her short story, "Tony Bennett, Aldous Huxley, and Eddie" won an Honorable Mention in the 205 Glimmer Train Short Fiction Contest. She blogs at stillinschool.wordpress.com.

CHRISTINE STODDARD is a Salvadoran-Scottish-American writer and artist who lives in Brooklyn. Her visuals have appeared in the New York Transit Museum, the Ground Zero Hurricane Katrina Museum, the Poe Museum, the Queens Museum, the Condé Nast Building, George Washington University's Gallery 102, and beyond. In 2014, Folio Magazine named her one of the top 20 media visionaries in their 20s for founding the culture magazine, Quail Bell. Christine's artwork has been recognized by the Puffin Foundation, Artbridge, and the Library of Virginia.

PAUL LUIKART'S first collection of short stories, Animal Heart, was released by Hyperborea Publishing in May 2016. Besides writing, he paints and draws. His MFA is from Seattle Pacific University. He and his family live in Chattanooga, Tennessee where he often feels like a round, liberal peg in a square, conservative hole.

MARK BLICKLEY AND AMY BASSIN'S video collaboration, Speaking In Bootongue, was selected for the London 2016 Experimental Film Festival. Their text-based art collaboration Dream Streams, was published in the Columbia Journal of Literature & Art, Mad Gleam Press, Vol. 11 Post[mortem], Three Rooms Press Maintenant: A Journal of Contemporary Dada Writing and Art Issues 9, 10, 11 and in many other publications as well as featured as an art installation at the 5th Annual NYC Poetry Festival on Governors Island. Bassin is a video artist/photographer from New York City and a graduate of the School of Visual Arts. Her works have been exhibited at Bronx ArtSpace, Photo Center Northwest, Exit Art Underground and Brooklyn's Ray Gallery. Blickley is the author of Sacred Misfits (Red Hen Press) and his most recent play, The Milkman's Sister, was produced at NYC's 13th Street Repertory Theater last Fall. He is a proud member of the Dramatists Guild and PEN American Center.

DMITRY BORSHCH was born in Dnepropetrovsk, studied in Moscow, today lives in New York. His drawings and sculptures have been exhibited at the National Arts Club (New York), Brecht Forum (New York), ISE Cultural Foundation (New York), the State Russian Museum (Saint Petersburg).

BRUCE HARRIS is the author of Sherlock Holmes and Dr. Watson: About Type

PHILLIP BANNOWSKY is a retired autoworker, international educator, human rights activist, and 2017 Delaware Division of the Arts Established Artist Fellow in poetry. Published works include The Milk of Human Kindness (poetry), Autoplant: a Poetic Monologue, and The Mother Earth Inn (novel). He is a contributing editor at Dreamstreets Magazine and Broadkill Review and curates Broken Turtle Booklist, which catalogues Delaware writers (brokenturtlebooks.com). Poems have appeared in Labor: Studies in Working Class History of the Americas, Currents, and The Moise A. Khayrallah Center for Lebanese Diaspora Studies News. He teaches the Poetry of Empowerment at the University of Delaware.
His contribution to this anthology is from Jacobo the Turko, a verse novel about an Ecuadorian of indigenous and Lebanese parentage who seeks the American Dream working a summer job in Delaware only to be deported to Lebanon (where he has never been), abducted to Bagram, and ultimately confined at Gitmo.

JOEL & VALERIE REEVES live in a small town in Northwest Lower Michigan where people get sent to the cornfield on a fairly regular basis. Joel's short stories have appeared in a variety of magazines and three of his fantasy novels were released by Double Dragon Press. Valerie's one-act play, The Dinner Party, was recently produced at the Traverse City Opera House. "Blunderland" is their first collaboration as a father-daughter writing team.

KENNETH NICHOLS earned his MFA in Creative Writing from Ohio State and maintains the writing craft website Great Writers Steal (www.greatwriterssteal.com). His work has appeared in a wide range of publications including Main Street Rag, Literary Orphans, and Lunch Ticket.

STEVE SMITH A lover of the desert as a result of growing up in El Paso, Texas, Steve Smith moved to Southeast Arizona after forty years in the cold winters of Michigan. He lives on a "ranchette" surrounded by mountains with wife Peggy, four cats and a dog, where he is polishing several novels, short stories and a humorous memoir of his peacetime Army days.

TYSON WEST lives in Eastern Washington with its beautiful vistas, dry dusty summers and cold winters on the bottom of the flood plain of the great Ice Age flood. He enjoys reciting his poetry to magpies and coyotes. He has a day job in real estate.

He has published poetry in Danse Macabre, Misfits Miscellany, Subtopian, Haiku Journal, 50 Haikus, Three Line Poetry, World Haiku Review, Cattails Haiku Journal, Quartrainfish Big Pulp, Cowboy Poetry Press, Annapurna, Akitsu Quarterly, the Quarterday Review, the Fib Review, Shot Glass Journal, and Scifaikuest. He has published sci-fi, horror and speculative stories in various anthologies. He has had two poems nominated for the Pushcart Prize. His poetry collection "Home-Canned Forbidden Fruit" is available from Gribble Press. His novella "Mall of the Damned" was published in 2014 by Red Dashboard Publishing, LLC.

MAVERICK SMITH is an LGBTQ+, Deaf, disabled settler who tackles themes of social justice and equity in their work. They are honored to be included in this anthology. Previously Maverick's work has been published or is forthcoming in several other anthologies including QDA: A Queer Disability Anthology, and Tripping the Tale Fantastic: Weird Fiction by Deaf and Hard of Hearing Writers. Maverick has also been a featured author at Naked Heart: An LGBTQ+ Festival of Words which was presented by Glad Day Bookshop.

ABOUT THE EDITORS

GABRIEL H. SANCHEZ

Gabriel H. Sanchez is an author, filmmaker, director, actor, and publisher from the Rio Grande Valley.
He is co-founder and editor at The Raving Press.

ISAAC CHAVARRIA

Isaac Chavarria still lives in Alton, TX and is currently working on his second manuscript of poetry, Moxado. His first poetry collection, Poxo, won the 2014 NACCS Tejas Poetry Prize.

FOR MORE INFORMATION VISIT

HTTP://WWW.THERAVINGPRESS.COM

www.ingramcontent.com/pod-product-compliance
Lightning Source LLC
Chambersburg PA
CBHW031656030726
47494CB00007BB/2213